MW01518262

Jen's Journey

Masters of the Prairie Winds Club

Book Three

by Avery Gale

Dedication

A big shout-out to the "real" Jen...your "sparkle" and sense of adventure made you the perfect inspiration and I thank you for all the giggles during our chats.

Dedication

A big shout-out to the "real" Jen...your "sparkle" and sense of adventure made you the perfect inspiration and I thank you for all the giggles during our chats.

Prologue

Almost one year later...

JAX MCDONALD LEANED back in the subtle leather wingback chair facing Kyle West's massive mahogany desk and listened as his best friend and their bosses discussed the fact Sam and Sage McCall had resigned their commissions with the SEALs and would be back on U.S. soil and looking for work soon. Kyle and his twin brother, Kent, had been teammates of Jax and his best friend, Micah Drake, during the entire time they'd been in the Special Forces, so joining them as a part of the security team for The Masters of the Prairie Winds Club while their own security business got up and running had been a natural transition. However, now that more of their brothers were transitioning out from under Uncle Sam's watch, they'd had several discussions like this one as they'd brainstormed different options.

The decision to hire Sage and Sam to become a part of Micah and Jax's security firm had been a no-brainer. The company had grown by leaps and bounds, and finding trained, qualified employees that you trusted with your life was never easy—unless you hired your former team members. There was no question there was plenty of work for the McCall brothers, and the raises and perks they'd offered them had sweetened the deal enough to get them to agree to relocate to Austin from their beloved Houston. The truth was, Jax was so grateful for their help getting a family friend safely out of Costa Rica last year that he'd been willing to offer them the moon if that had been necessary.

Jen Keating had inadvertently come onto the radar of Raphael Baldamino, the same man who had held Jax and Micah's new wife, Gracie, captive over a decade ago. Baldamino had planned to make Jen the blonde opposite of Gracie's soft Latino beauty. He'd ordered her abduction after seeing her picture, but the fools he'd hired had gotten the wrong woman. Granted, Danielle Brandt and Jen looked enough alike to be sisters, their mistake had bought Jax's friends enough time to prevent her becoming another human trafficking victim statistic.

They'd all had a huge scare last year when a single red rose had been delivered to Gracie on the beach in San Diego. As long as he lived, Jax would never forget the terror he'd felt as he'd seen a crowd gathering around he and Micah's fiancée as they'd raced jet skis just off shore. By the time they'd made their way to her side she was just regaining consciousness and his heart had nearly stopped when he'd felt the fear pulsing from her. She'd been white as a ghost and shaking like a leaf despite the warm temperature. They'd launched an immediate search for the man who'd delivered the flower but hadn't ever found him. The waiter who'd made the delivery was also a full-time art student and he'd been able to provide a tremendous amount of detail as well as drawing a sketch of the man who'd made the request. Gracie hadn't recognized the man and that had eased her mind tremendously. They'd finally been forced to view the incident as a man simply wanting to make contact with a beautiful woman despite the fact

he'd assured the waiter she'd know who the flower was from.

In the back of Jax's mind he heard Kyle say, "Sam called late last night to say they'd be on leave until separation as soon as they get home from the mission they are packing out for. They are about to go wheels up because there's been a situation at an American Embassy, hostages involved including a civilian language specialist." *What the fuck!*

Jax's attention riveted on Kyle and he snapped, "What did you just say? What embassy? Did he tell you?" Jax knew that was unlikely given the secretive nature of the work the SEALs did, but he could only hope Sam had given him a good enough clue, then they could figure it out.

Kyle's brow wrinkled and he studied Jax for a second, "You know he couldn't tell me that. But he did remind me how much he loves Pez candy and how we'd enjoyed them together shortly before Kent and I got out." Kyle paused and Jax saw a grin spread over his face before he continued, "So I'd say he's headed to La Paz since we were all there not so long ago."

Jax froze and felt the hair on the back of his neck stand up on end. "Fuck! Hang on." Grabbing his phone, he typed in a short message to his younger sister, Elza, before returning his attention to Kyle, Kent, and Micah. "Jen was headed there the last time I talked to mom, and God knows if she was anywhere in or around the area when this went down, but she's likely right in the middle of the chaos. Christ the little trouble magnet is going to give me a fucking ulcer and she isn't even my blood sister. Fuck me. I swear the woman needs a damned keeper." Swiping his hand over his face in frustration, he finally spoke again after several deep breaths. "I don't want to call my parents until

I've heard from Elza, but if I don't hear from her in a few minutes I will. Do you have any way to get word to them? Give them a head's up if we find out she's involved?"

They all knew walking into a situation like this, where one of the victims knew a rescuer personally, was a recipe for disaster. Not only was there too much personal emotion attached to the situation muddling everyone's judgment, but it also meant the lightning fast decisions involved in hostage rescues were much more difficult to make as well. If they knew she was there, they could make allowances that might well save all of their lives.

Jax shook his head as he considered what might be coming. "Look, I know she turned their world upside down before they'd even gotten her back on U.S. soil last year. Hell, she'd been a handful as long as I've known her, but she really is solid. She just attracts trouble like a fucking neodymium magnet."

Kent had whistled softly and Jax had seen Micah's hands tighten on the armrests of the chair he was sitting in. Kyle leaned forward and started typing into his phone and once he'd finished he looked up and smiled, "And that isn't even taking into account the pandemonium she wrecked at your wedding reception. Holy hell, I've never seen Sam McCall so totally unhinged."

Jax shook his head as he remembered the insanity of that evening. The memory alone made him cringe every time it came to mind. Jen had been tipsy before the reception had even started, but sometime during their photo shoot she'd gone way over the edge into fully inebriated. He should have sent her to her suite at the hotel before the dinner, but he'd hoped getting some food in her stomach would settle her down. He'd been wrong.

"Don't remind me. Hell, my mom barely spoke to me

for a couple of months—you'd have thought I'd personally arranged her little Jell-O shooters party with Elza and their sorority sisters."

Kent leaned forward and chuckled, "Well, it certainly became clear she hadn't really dealt with all the fallout from Costa Rica as well as we'd all thought. Never ceases to amaze me how long that shit can fester before it bubbles to the top." Jax agreed with Kent's assessment, but it didn't change the fact Jen's behavior had been way over the top and totally out of character. The explanation hadn't changed the fact the little vixen had gotten to the McCall brothers in a very big way and then waltzed out of the hotel at the ass crack of dawn the next morning without so much as a goodbye. She'd hopped a plane to DC, accepted a job with the State Department later that day as a language specialist, and had essentially cut herself off from everyone.

Looking down at his phone when it vibrated in his hand, Jax groaned when he read the message from his younger sister, Elza. "La Paz – Why?" *FUBAR is going to be the understatement of the century, because this mess is about to be as fucked up beyond all recognition as it can get.* Looking up, he simply nodded and every man around him sprang into action. Micah bumped his shoulder and said, "Come on." Jax knew his friend was headed to their security offices, which were about a half mile from the club because they'd be more effective using their own equipment even though Micah had set up the control center at the club as well. And truthfully, neither one liked leaving Gracie alone too long anyway. Just thinking about their new bride brought a rush of warmth to his heart.

As they made their way out of the Wests' office, Kent grasped his shoulder halting his progress. "Try not to worry about her, we'll get word to the McCalls. I swear if they don't put a collar on her and paddle her ass I'm gonna string them both up by their short and curlies." Jax felt himself relax just a bit and nodded his agreement, he really did appreciate his friend's attempt to lighten the moment. He caught up with Micah just as he started the John Deere Gator they'd ridden to the club in. Between the two small ranches, they had a small fleet of Gators that had been specially modified, including sensors and souped up engines.

Once they'd moved into their new home and office building at the front of Kent and Kyle's parents place next to the club, they'd cut a trail through the trees and modified the fence that separated the properties. It had started as a safety backup for their women but like many do-it-yourself projects tackled by ultra-techy former SEALs, it had spiraled out of control quickly. The end result was a fence packing enough voltage to stun even the strongest man into a quivering state of helplessness. There was an automatic gate with sensors that would only open for certain vehicles—if the sensors didn't receive the right signal, everything locked up tight. If the system locked, the electric current began pulsing both down to the ground and up several feet in the air, they'd wanted to be sure no one decided to crawl under or hurdle the damned thing. Was it overkill? Maybe, but as Lilly West had said, "Boys will be boys and they do so love their toys."

GRACIE LISTENED TO the Gator zip by the back hedge and park in the garage. She'd known her husbands would be home from their meeting with Kent and Kyle West soon, but she hadn't been able to manage enough energy to get out of the lounger where she'd been soaking up the last rays of the afternoon's warm sunshine. She'd felt like she was battling the flu for several days and since it hadn't seemed to have gotten worse, she'd decided an afternoon of rest was probably all it would take to kick whatever bug she'd come into contact with to the curb. Lord of Leapers she had no intention of letting Jax or Micah know she was feeling punk, they'd summon specialists from all around the country to examine her. *Gotta love 'em. Overprotective as they are, they're mine and I love them with everything in me.*

Just as she'd started to doze again, she felt familiar fingers brush her bangs aside with a gentle caress. *Micah.* In the beginning, she'd wondered how she could tell them apart by their touch, but Lilly had assured her that souls recognize one another on a deep level that defies explanation. So she'd just let the question go and enjoyed the fact it was true. "My love, what's wrong? And don't you dare try to tell me nothing." Feeling the cool of his shadow fall over her face, she let her eyes flutter open without squinting. He obviously read the question in her eyes because he laughed softly, "Baby, did you think your Masters hadn't notice you were feeling under the weather?"

Her soft, "Oh" hadn't really been an answer to either of his questions, so he just watched her and waited patiently. "I'm sorry, I wasn't trying to be secretive...I just didn't want you to worry. I think I have a bug, I just feel a bit blah, you know?"

"And?" Taking a deep breath, she tried to will the words to the surface but there were times her old insecurities seemed dangerously close to catching up with her, and this moment was one of those. "Still struggling with letting go of the notion you have to handle everything alone, aren't you, little subbie?" Micah feathered his fingers under her eyes and she already knew what he was seeing, because the bruising under her skin from not sleeping well was getting harder and harder to conceal. She'd eaten lunch with Regi, the club's resident wonder office administrator, and she'd even remarked that Gracie seemed awfully tired. Frustration and a feeling of not being in control started to overwhelm her and Gracie knew the tears she'd been battling were close to breaking free of her tenuous grasp.

"I'm sorry, I just didn't want you to drag me to a bunch of doctors. It's just a touch of the flu and I hate being a bother when I know you all are working so hard on plans for expanding." She hadn't actually intended to share that much information but now it was out there, she sure couldn't pull the words back.

"Bet you didn't mean to spill all of that did you, sweetness? Oh, don't look so surprised, it was written all over your face. Yes, we have been busy, but we will *never* be too busy to care for you." He continued stroking the sides of her face, then leaned forward and kissed her on the forehead. "Have you considered the possibility you might be pregnant, love?" Gracie felt the blood drain from her face. The thought had never occurred to her...it hadn't been on her radar at all. She saw the amusement in his face, but the blood was pounding in her ears so loud she couldn't make out what else he was saying. Gracie felt him slide his arms under her and lift her onto his lap. "No, I can see you hadn't actually considered that possibility, had you? Well, I want you to know that we have, and honestly we're hoping like hell that is exactly what this is about."

Micah just held her for several minutes until she'd settled down and when she leaned back and looked up into his eyes, the love shining from them touched her soul. "I'm sorry I panicked. Where is Jax?"

"He's making some calls, seems Miss Jen has likely found herself in a pickle again." Gracie froze and waited for him to continue. She hadn't gotten to spend a lot of time with Jen, but she'd been drawn to her and if given the opportunity, they'd be great friends. Thinking Jen had gotten herself in the thick of things again sent shivers through Gracie. Micah stood with her still cradled in his arms as if she weighed nothing at all. "Well, now that you seem to be a little steadier, let's get you inside. A nice warm bath for you while Jax and I tie up a few loose ends and then I do believe we'll tie you up and see where that leads us. What do you say?"

She giggled and pressed her lips against his neck, "That sounds perfect…Master."

Chapter One

JEN SAT ON the cold stone floor beneath the embassy and fumed. *Fucking ass wads. I paid a lot of money for this outfit and sitting on this moldy floor is not helpful. And what the hell is their issue with me anyway?* It had been obvious from the time the embassy had been stormed the men had known exactly who she was. Even though she had refused to acknowledge their repeated inquiries. In her opinion if they were too dimwitted to read the State Department identification card clipped to the lanyard around her neck, then they could go jump. It had been difficult to pretend she didn't understand Spanish, but for once her finely honed skills as a ditsy blonde had paid off.

As a teenager, Jen had always struggled to fit in because she'd been shuttled between the various accelerated programs in different schools and had rarely been with anyone her own age. Her Mensa level IQ hadn't been discovered until her freshman year of high school, after that her social circle had essentially dwindled to her instructors and her foster mother. The stab of pain that went through her heart whenever she thought about Millie Sinclair almost made her double over. Being moved into Millie's home had been the biggest blessing Jen could have ever asked for. And when the sweet woman had died suddenly a couple of months before Jen turned eighteen, the only thing that had kept her from being turned over to yet another state agency had been Bill and Carol McDonald's intervention.

Jen had been hired as a liaison of sorts for their daughter, Elza. The freshman girl had been struggling to adapt to college life because she was deaf and just negotiating the administrative system alone was difficult when none of the college staff signed. She and Elza shared an advisor and the young professor knew Jen was proficient in American Sign Language so it had been an easy match. What had been a surprise to everyone was what a godsend that pairing would turn into.

Elza was one of the sweetest people Jen had ever met and they'd bonded almost from the first moment they met. And even though her parents were wealthy beyond Jen's comprehension, Elza had never been a diva or difficult to work with. The first time Jen had visited the McDonald Mansion outside of Austin she'd been so nervous she'd nearly turned around and headed back down the long drive to the iron-gated entrance without even slowing down. Elza had bounded down the enormous front staircase, her smile as wide as Jen had ever seen, her hands signing so fast Jen hadn't even been able to keep up with her enthusiastic friend.

Pulling her legs up so she could rest her head on her arms, Jen turned her face from the men who sat staring at her from across the room. They'd released a few of the hostages when several had pointed out they were actually locals who didn't deserve to be caught up in whatever issues the intruders had with the American staff. Jen had been scheduled to leave La Paz first thing in the morning and now the decision to stay an extra day and help the Ambassador with his special project seemed a little too coincidental for her liking. *If that twiddle-dicked midget sold me out I swear I'll kick his ass, tie him up in some of those fancy-assed knots the McCall brothers used on me, and drop his worthless self into Lake Titicaca.* Jen snorted to herself, how fitting that a dweeb should land in a body of water named after words Americans associated with boobs and crap.

Jen had taken an instant dislike to Christian Felps, but her job with the State Department had been to assess the people the weasel had been negotiating with, not the man her boss had sent to run the embassy. She'd done her best to avoid being alone with him after she'd had to fend off numerous sexual advances, but he'd seemed to have a way of catching her anytime she was by herself in the com-pound. The fact she'd been within minutes of leaving for her hotel when his office had been stormed seemed an odd turn of events, but it was downright unnerving that he hadn't been taken hostage. Everyone knew that an ambassador held more negotiating power than a lowly linguist did. And it wasn't difficult to see she was actually the focus of most of the attention.

Knowing the news of the takeover would likely have already made its way to the McDonalds caused her heart to squeeze tight. Bill and Carol McDonald had been so supportive over the years, they'd practically adopted her, and the thought that she'd once again be causing them worry made her heartsick. After the fiasco in Costa Rica and then her unforgiveable behavior at their son's wedding, Jen worried they might finally wash their hands of her for good.

Jen had wondered a thousand times over the past seven months why she'd been so set on a course of self-destruction the night of Jax, Gracie, and Micah's wedding, and the only thing she'd ever been able to deduce was that she'd just simply been bat shit crazy. After the whole debacle in Costa Rica, and her foolishness on the way back to Texas, she'd been completely unprepared for the feelings that had exploded inside her heart when Sam and Sage McCall had walked into the ballroom after the ceremony. When she'd casually asked Elza several weeks earlier which of her brother's teammates would be attending the ceremony, her insightful friend had looked at her with sad brown eyes and had shaken her head. Elza had explained the McCall brothers were out of the country and weren't supposed to be home for several months, so Jen hadn't had time to shore up her emotional defenses in preparation for their appearance.

Holy Henry and Hannah she'd made such a fool of herself that night. Even now she could barely wrap her mind around everything that had happened. Sneaking into the hotel's bar for a few Jell-O shooters with her sorority sisters had seemed like a great way to numb her mind, but things had quickly spiraled out of control. Dancing on the marble-topped bar had been a straight-up *Coyote Ugly* moment up until she'd fallen off backwards and landed in Sam McCall's waiting arms.

Remembering how heartsick she'd felt when she'd seen the frustration in Jax's eyes and the disappointment in Carol's was nearly her undoing. The salty taste of a teardrop tracked the seam of her lips before running down her arm. Jen buried her face in her arms and tried to refocus her thoughts away from the guilt and humiliation of that night. *Damn and double damn. I hate to cry.*

SAM MCDONALD WAS surprised to see an urgent message on his Sat phone from Kyle West when they landed in La

Paz. It was short but had taken his breath away. Passing it over to his brother, he watched Sage's eyes go wide just before he growled, "I'm gonna beat her ass." Yeah, Sam could totally relate. Detouring to the customer service desk to retrieve the package Jax had said was waiting for them, Sam's mind was full throttle ahead as he considered all the ramifications of what he'd just learned.

The screen on the phone dimmed as Sam stared at the words *'J Keating one of your snatch and grabs – Pkg at Cust Srvs'* until they faded completely from his view. How on earth had the woman who had shaken both he and his brother to their very cores manage to get herself into another mess? The first time his fingers had touched her arm in the hallway of her hotel in Costa Rica he'd felt an arc of electricity move through him, and he had barely been able to think of anything but the little blonde whose mind was even quicker than her sharp tongue, though not by much.

A man didn't have to talk to Jen Keating long before her brilliance was glaringly obvious. Sam wasn't sure he'd ever met anyone who could process information on so many levels at the same time. As a sexual Dominant, he had already known just how difficult it was for women like that to ever silence their minds. The noise inside their heads was often deafening and usually drained them until nothing but exhaustion remained. He'd talked to many professional women who were also submissives and they'd assured him the escape they found in submission had saved their sanity more than once.

Sam hadn't fully understood until three years ago when he'd spoken with the owner of a club in Houston and his submissive. CeCe was a widely successful surgeon, she had started a surgical center that was one of the best known in the entire world, and a sexual slave to her Dom husband the minute she walked out of her clinic. Sam and Sage had known Cameron Barnes for years because their parents had been friends since the boys had all been in diapers, so Sam had asked Cam for permission to speak freely with CeCe during dinner one evening.

Cam had summoned the naked buxom beauty from her position at his feet and settled her on his lap, he'd instructed her that she was free of her regular protocols with guests until he rescinded the order. He'd cautioned her that even though she was to be candid, she should also be respectful in her answers. Sam had seen her blush making him wonder what had happened in the past that had made Cam bring that fact to her attention. Hell, the woman was one of the best-trained subs he'd ever met, he couldn't imagine she'd ever given Cam a moment's trouble, but maybe...

His friend had merely smiled and said, "I can see it written all over your face, my friend. And yes, even my lovely pet misbehaves occasionally, and even though I believe her comments to the abusive Dom she gave a thorough tongue lashing a few months ago were completely justified and spot-on, the fact was she was intolerably rude. She was punished for her presentation of the facts, not the facts themselves. And I'm guessing the punishment isn't something she is likely to forget anytime soon, nor do I believe it's an issue we'll need to revisit in the foreseeable future."

Sam didn't even want to think about what Cam had come up with as a punishment for his lovely slave because the man was an evil genius who lived for chances to design new ways to push a subs boundaries. They'd spent the next hour listening as CeCe had explained exactly what it was like inside her head when she was in professional mode and how her submission to Cam was the only peace she'd ever known. Sam had never considered intelligence a curse until CeCe had explained it, unfortunately, it doesn't come with an on-off switch so quieting the thoughts was a constant challenge. When she hadn't been convinced he and Sage were comprehending, she'd asked Cam's permission to do a quick demo and he'd agreed.

For several minutes they'd watched as Cam's naked slave had moved around their penthouse gathering anything that would make noise. She'd carefully tuned each device to a different channel and then asked them to step into the middle of the room. When they'd joined her, CeCe had handed them a puzzle and a pencil and asked them to complete it as quickly as possible and then she'd turned the volume up until he'd worried their various art pieces were going to tumble to the polished marble floors. It had taken both he and Sage almost ten minutes to complete the relatively simple puzzle, and even though they were highly trained SEALs they had both found it nearly impossible to function with so much distraction.

When CeCe had explained that what they'd experienced was what her life was like outside of her life with her Master, Sam and Sage had both marveled at how she functioned day in and day out. Now, thinking about Jen and what Jax had told them about how incredibly bright she was, he had to wonder if it hadn't been that "white noise" as CeCe had termed it, which was haunting her. The tiny tornado seemed to be on a path set to self-detonate in the near future and when they pulled her sweet ass out of the fire this time, he fully intended to light it right up again the minute he and Sage got her alone.

SAGE HAD LOOKED at Sam's phone and fought to keep from grinding his teeth to dust. *How does she do it? How in bloody hell does a woman as smart as Jen Keating keep landing herself in the thick of things? Jesus, Joseph, and Mary, who's going to pull her back from the fucking edge after we leave the team?* The thought of another operative being sent out to rescue her in the future sent his blood into a rolling boil.

The woman had gotten to both he and Sam in a huge way after they'd agreed to help former teammate, Jax McDonald, out when he'd sent out an SOS requesting help getting a family friend out of Costa Rica. The family friend turned out to be a ball of fire who had incinerated both he and Sam. They'd rescued her just as she'd been accosted in the hallway outside her hotel room and then she'd come apart at the seams when they'd insisted she only pack the barest of essentials so they could get her out of the building before the jokers they'd knocked out were MIA long enough to attract attention. The fact she'd taken the term "barest essentials" quite literally and begun throwing in lacy bras and see-thru thongs had sent enough blood to his cock he'd actually been lightheaded for a few seconds.

Sam had been the one to point out to her that her backpack, jeans, jacket, shoes, and computer were probably more important than her Victoria's Secret stash. Sage smiled to himself as he remembered the look on her face when he'd raked the entire contents of the bathroom counter into her bag in one swift swipe. Hell, for a few seconds he'd thought her head was going to start spinning around on her slender shoulders. Her squeaked question, "What the fuck was that about?" had gotten her a swat to her ass from Sam. When she'd spun on him, Sam had quickly pulled her tight into his arms trapping her against his much larger frame.

Sage had leaned down, pressed his lips against her ear, and commanded, "*Stop. Now*. We know you are trained in self-defense, but we are as well and we're a lot bigger than you are, sweet cheeks, and a hell of a lot meaner. Now get your sweet ass in gear so we can clear out." Her reaction to his command and Sam's restraint had been mesmerizing, the woman was a born submissive, even though convincing her would probably be hair-raising torture. *God, I love the sassy ones.*

The memory of her, naked between them in the bedroom on board the McDonalds' private jet, would be etched in his memory until his dying breath. The silky softness of her skin brushing against him had made every cell in his body sit up and sing the Halleluiah Chorus. Sage had circled her nipples with his tongue until they'd been tight little berries ripe for picking. When he'd tightened his teeth around them, just enough to make her squeak, her legs had instinctively widened and Sam had been right there waiting. Watching his brother bury his face in her waxed pussy had been pure eroticism, but her uninhibited reactions were what tested every bit of his control.

Seeing her blonde hair fanned out over the dark pillow as she arched off the bed had awakened a part of Sage's soul he hadn't even known existed until that moment. Hell, he'd been sexually active since he'd been a teenager and he'd never reacted to a woman the way he had to Jen. There was just a purity and goodness about her that seemed to radiate from the depth of her soul, and there hadn't been a doubt in his mind that with Jen Keating, the woman you saw was exactly who she was.

Now they were a part of a small team being sent in to pull the little tigress out of the fire once again. Going in to a hostile situation had inherent dangers, but stepping into a room where one of the victims knew the rescuer personally brought a plethora of new concerns. Sam was their lead on this mission, so technically it was his call if they stood down and let the others enter first, but Sage didn't doubt for a single moment that wasn't going to happen. There was no way either he or Sam would let another man rescue the woman who had worked herself under their skin a year ago. *Damn it to hell, why can't I get her out of my head?*

Sage had been captivated from the first moment he'd laid eyes on her. She'd swung out of the hotel's revolving glass door into the sunshine in her strappy sandals and sundress, and Sage's heart had nearly stopped beating. Seeing the sun sparkle off her long blonde hair and the dewy moisture making her tanned skin glow had shaken him. He'd known Jax's younger sister had been assigned a student mentor when she'd been in college and he'd known the entire McDonald family had essentially adopted her, but he'd never actually seen Jen Keating until that moment. And holy fucking hell what a moment it had been.

Sam's voice jarred his thoughts back to the moment at hand, "Hey, you gonna be able to keep your head out of the clouds long enough to get this done?"

"Fuck you. Has the plan changed?"

"No. ETA is ten. Look at this map again; I want it executed perfectly. Don't let her derail you, and we both know she is more than capable. Hell, the woman would distract a eunuch." Sam's voice was a near growl and that got the attention of the other guys sitting in the back of the junker delivery truck they were using as transport. The only way

19

they would get near the embassy was if their vehicle looked like it was bringing the supplies demanded by the goons holding the hostages. Their orders were to go in clean and out as clean as possible. The powers that be had gone impossibly soft if anyone asked either he or Sam, and that had been one of the things that tipped the scales for them to resign their commissions. *And isn't it a laugh riot that our final mission is to rescue the other reason.*

Chapter Two

J EN WAS EXHAUSTED and starving, and that had always been an almost certain recipe for disaster for her. Either state could send her into orbit, but the combination made her pissy on a good day and was threatening to make her downright homicidal today. She had listened to the two thugs standing guard on the other side of the room as they'd debated how long it was going to be until their dinner arrived until she'd been ready to snatch them both bald. They didn't seem at all concerned about the three people they still held captive. The other two women looked like they were barely eighteen and Jen wondered why the Ambassador had been willing to hire women that young when common sense alone should have indicated the potential political fallout could be devastating. *Hell's bells had everybody forgotten about Monica Lewinsky? Jesus, talk about a lesson for every politician on the planet.* The young White House intern who had nearly brought down an American Presidency single handedly and had made fools of all the "doubters" because she'd been wily enough to save the evidence of her tryst with the good Pres. *Well, single-handed isn't quite right, I'm pretty sure her mouth was involved in that one as well.*

Realizing her bladder was tired of being ignored, Jen decided to continue playing the meek, frightened victim card and asked sweetly to use the restroom. When the men protested, she stood and started to dance around and gave crying her best effort until they finally relented. The captors' English wasn't the best, but it wasn't the worst either so she planned to continue pretending she couldn't understand any of their Spanish bickering about who was going to accompany the Albino bitch to the latrine. Jen thanked her guardian angel when the smaller of the two men stepped forward and motioned her out the door with his rifle.

Even though she'd had weapons training when she'd joined the department, Jen had never seen anything that looked remotely like the gun he was carrying. If she had to guess, she'd put her money on World War II leftovers. *Geez, with the lucrative drug markets in this part of the world you'd think his boss would at least get him a gun from the Vietnam era.* Once they got to the small bathroom, Jen knew the real struggle was about to begin.

When he started to follow her inside, she halted him and shook her head no. She swung the door wide open and pointed around the interior, "See? No windows and no doors. Where would I go? I just want to pee and wash my hands. That's all."

The asshat must have been satisfied because he'd stepped back, and snapped, "I be waiting. Go fast." She'd nodded, barely resisting the urge to give him a mocking salute and ducked inside and flipped the lock on the heavy wooden door. *Moron.* Jen had just finished washing her hands when she heard a loud thump against the door, stepping to the side she looked for something, anything, to use as a weapon and the only thing she found was a spray can of air freshener. Shrugging, she grabbed it, positioned herself behind the door, and waited.

SAM HAD BEEN surprised at how few men there were guarding the small embassy compound, something that reeked of an inside job in his view. Hell, it had taken them less than a minute to make their way into the main building and into the dank basement. The clown standing outside the restroom hadn't even heard them descend the stairs and with one well-placed move he'd been dispatched and dropped like a stone. As he'd secured the thug in flexi-cuffs, the rest of his team had moved down the hall. They'd quickly dispatched the other captor and left Sage to secure the man while they led two women out of the building...neither women was the sassy sprite he'd expected to see. Suddenly realizing why the man had been guarding the bathroom door, Sam moved back down the hall and pulled on the handle. Locked.

Cursing under his breath, "Fuck. Can't anything be easy with her?" He gave the door a solid kick with his boot and sent it flying inward just as he found himself in a mist of some sort of sickeningly sweet spray that made his damned eyes water and stole his breath. "Goddammit, what the fuck? Jen?"

He heard her gasp, "Sam?"

"Yeah, doll. Mind telling me what that was about." He'd barely managed to cough out the words before she'd launched herself at his chest wrapping her arms and legs around him like a spider monkey. For just one heartbeat he relished the feel of her small body pressed against his and was keenly aware of the fact her sex was pressing against his rapidly inflating cock. His big head had finally come back on-line and when his training kicked in, he'd sprinted toward the exit.

It was a damned good thing this was his last mission because there was no way he'd ever live down coming out of a snatch and grab smelling like he'd taken a walk through his sweet granny's flower garden. *I hope like hell this shit washes off or it's gonna be a long fucking ride to the airport.*

Stepping outside into a deluge, Sam was grateful for the impromptu shower, but knew immediately there was no way their transport would be taking off anytime soon, so they'd be switching to their backup plan for evacuating any Americans who wanted out. Stepping into the back of the truck with Jen still clinging to him, he turned to his brother, "How many are we taking?"

"Just her. The other girls were locals and refused any further help. The place is secure for now." Sage's words might have been purely professional, but his expression was anything but. He'd leaned close and whispered against Jen's ear, "You okay, sweet cheeks?" Her face was pressed against Sam's neck but he'd felt her quick nod. Sage looked at him, "She need a medic? If not, we need to get the hell out of Dodge because the other two women indicated they believed Jen was the original target."

Sam knew he hadn't hidden his anger when the other men looked at him with raised brows. Waving them off, he started trying to pry her arms from their locked position around his neck so he could look at her. "Come on, Jen. Let me get a look at you. We need to make sure you are alright." She finally eased her hold and pulled back enough for him to become lost in the most beautiful crystal blue eyes he's ever seen. God, how had he forgotten how easy they were to fall into? He'd seen every ocean and many of the seas the good earth had to showcase, but he'd never seen a single body of water that could match the sparkling depth of color of Jen's eyes. When she finally let him put a few more inches between them he brushed her hair aside and smiled. "That's a good girl. Now, did they hurt you?" He felt a flood of relief when she shook her head. "When is the last time you ate?"

He could tell the last question had surprised her, but she'd recovered quickly and answered, "I'm not sure, really…yesterday afternoon, I think." His Dominant nature nearly exploded through his surface calm. *How dare she not take better care of herself? Well that fucking changes as of this moment.* He took the small bottle of water Sage passed him and unscrewed the lid before handing it to her. His brother's stern look told Sam he wasn't happy with her response either.

Carl Phillips was one of the best SEAL teammates Sam had ever worked with, but the man drove like an Indy racer so they were all being tossed around in the back of the truck like peas in a boxcar. Just as Sam opened his mouth to ask him what the rush was, he noticed lights behind them. Sage was already digging through the open bag at his feet and Sam watched as his brother slid the slim titanium bracelet around Jen's wrist and locked it into place before she had even had a chance to question him. There were only two keys to the small lock, and he and Sage were each wearing one around their necks. How Jax had managed to have the high tech tracking device waiting for them when they'd arrived was just another one of the mysteries of the universe Sam didn't have time to figure out.

"What is this? Where did you get it? What does it do?" *Oh yeah, there she is, there's the bold, questioning woman we met in Costa Rica.*

"Glad to see that brilliant mind is coming back on-line

25

so quickly, doll." Nodding to her wrist, he continued, "That is a gift from Jax, it will help us find you if we get separated for any reason." He caught her chin with his fingers and forced her to focus on his face before he continued, "We don't plan on needing it, so I want you to just consider it a very expensive piece of jewelry for now, understand? It's important that you not think about it as anything else. If you do, you may unconsciously pay particular attention to it, and even the most subtle attention wouldn't be missed by someone who wanted to hurt you. Do you understand?"

Watching her eyes dilate as she listened to his instructions was one of the sexiest things he'd ever seen. Here she was obviously physically and emotionally spent to the point of exhaustion, there was no question she had to be famished, and she still reacted to his Dom voice as only a true submissive would. *She's fucking perfect. And she's ours.*

Chapter Three

JEN STOOD IN the small bathroom of the seedy hotel they'd checked into and shivered, despite the fact the room was fast closing in on becoming a sauna. It hadn't taken the SEALs long to lose the Jeep that had been following them. *Note to self…never—ever—ride anywhere with Carl Phillips unless I'm trying to outrun bad guys.* Holy hairballs the man had some serious driving issues, but he'd gotten them safely to a small hotel not far from the airport, so Jen figured she should just count her blessings and call it a day. The water in the shower had been running for several minutes and was just beginning to feel lukewarm. "I swear the first thing I'm going to do when I get back to my apartment is kiss my water heater."

"What was that, sweet cheeks?" Jen would have smacked her forehead in exasperation if she'd had the energy. Great, she should have known that as soon as she started talking to herself one of the McCall brothers would be standing just outside the door.

"Um, nothing. I was just muttering to myself." Pulling back the shower curtain, she shrieked as a cockroach the size of a small bus scurried up the wall. The door slammed open and Sage stepped in front of her scanning the shower before turning back to her. Looking up into his dark eyes nearly gave her a case of vertigo, even though she had to lean her head back to see into his face, the feeling of falling forward into his gaze made her head spin.

"Whoa. Hold on, sweet cheeks. Here, sit down for a minute." He'd put a towel on the closed lid of the toilet before settling her onto it. "Do not move, got it?" When she nodded, he stepped out and she could hear him telling the others she was alright and they'd be out before Sam returned with their food. Returning to the small bath, he unbuckled his gun belt and set it aside before stripping quickly.

"Wait. What are you doing? I can't take a shower with you." Jen silently cursed the fact her protest had sounded weak, even to her own ears.

"And why would that be?" The corners of his mouth looked like they were turning up in amusement, but she was trying so hard to perfect her scowl that she wasn't sure. "It won't be the first time we've been wet together, sweetness." This time it was easy to see the devilment in his eyes and it made her want to roll hers. But she remembered all too vividly what the results of that had been in her hotel suite after Jax, Gracie, and Micah's wedding reception, and it seemed foolish to tempt fate again. Damn, her ass had been tender for several days and the thought of the long flights ahead of her kept her from wanting to repeat the experience.

The paddling they'd given her for her bratty behavior had both infuriated her and ignited a curiosity and passion she'd barely been managing to contain for years. Thinking about the hundreds of erotic romance novels she'd read and all the times she'd wondered how it would feel to be the heroine caught between two demanding Doms was not a good plan when she was facing the very impressive and rapidly hardening cock of one of the most attractive men she'd ever known. *Boy oh boy, I wonder if he really does taste as good as I remember or if my mind has manufactured a memory that is better than reality...because, I really hate it when that happens. Maybe I can lean forward and just take a quick taste and...*

Blinking back to the moment, Jen realized Sage had knelt in front of her so they were face to face. *Kind of a pity, really.* "Baby, that little mental field trip you just went on is part of what concerns me. I'm worried you're headed for an adrenaline crash of Biblical proportions and I'd just as soon we didn't have to stitch up any of your lovely body parts after you kissed the concrete." Once again he was standing in front of her with his legs spread apart in a no nonsense stance, totally unembarrassed by his nakedness. *And why the hell should he be? Leaping lizards the man is cut like a Greek God.* It seemed as if her eyes had decided to play hooky from her brain as they zeroed in on his erect cock and the pearly drop at the very tip. She hadn't even realized she'd licked her lips until she heard him growl.

"Fuck, woman. You're going to be the death of me. Come here." He grabbed her hands and pulled her to her feet before scooping her up and setting her over the edge of the large cast iron tub. Stepping in so he faced her, he moved her back until the warm water sprayed against the back of her head soaking her hair before cascading down her back and the rolling over her ass in whispering rivulets that were teasing her entire body to attention. "Lean back, sweetness. Let's get you nice and wet." His double innuendo hadn't been lost on her, and when she did as he'd told her, he leaned down and kissed the tip of her nose. "Good girl. I'm going to help you so I don't worry about having to rush in to rescue you from some enormous insect or rodent." She appreciated his attempt to lighten the mood between them and smiled up at him. He quickly lathered up her long hair with the small bottle of shampoo he'd pulled from his bag before he'd sent her in to shower.

His strong fingers massaged her scalp making her moan at the pleasure his hands were bringing. She'd always loved having someone else wash her hair, hell, that was absolutely the best part of her monthly haircuts in her opinion. "You like that, sweetness?" Sage's voice had become raspy and she'd have opened her eyes to answer but she was too lost in the bliss his touch was creating, she just couldn't manage to lift her eyelids. When she finally managed to groan, he'd chuckled, "I'll take that as a yes." He'd continued moving his hand through the wet strands of her hair and she let out a little yelp of surprise when he licked first one nipple and then the other. "You are so beautiful. I've dreamt about your soft skin and the beautiful curves of these perfect breasts, sweet cheeks. Your nipples are the sweetest rosy pink color. And remembering the way your sweet pussy felt squeezing my cock as you screamed my name has fueled every single fantasy I've had for the past year."

Feeling his lips brushing reverently over her skin was like setting a match to gasoline and she was suddenly much more interested in an entirely different kind of relief. Arching her back in an attempt to press her breasts against his chest was purely instinct driven. Sage leaned back, and when he rolled both of her nipples between his fingers until they were tight buds she felt herself sway against him just before her knees folded out from under her. Thank heaven he'd moved one of his arms and wrapped it around her waist or she'd have collapsed into the tub. "Come on, sweetness. Let's get you out of here. I promise Sam and I will give your body the relief it is craving, but first we need to get you warm and fed."

SAGE WANTED TO howl in victory at the way Jen had responded to his touch as he'd washed her hair. When he'd run his soapy hands up and down her arms he'd felt her shiver beneath his fingers. And when she'd leaned toward him as he'd repeated the soapy massage up and down both legs, it had taken every ounce of self-discipline he had to keep from pressing his mouth against her waxed sex and giving her the orgasm her body had been chasing. Though he knew she would have enjoyed the release immensely— he'd have seen that she'd come hard enough to scream his name—that wasn't how he and his brother wanted to begin with her. The plan was to work together until the relationship was well established. They both understood the value of one-on-one time in a permanent polyamorous relationship, but they also knew in the beginning they needed to present a united front.

In the back of his mind he'd heard he and Sam's friend and mentor, Cameron Barnes, repeating what they'd joked must be his mantra. *Begin as you intend to go* might not have been what his cock had wanted to hear, but as a trained Dom, Sage prided himself on having more control than giving in to a quick fuck in a pathetically antiquated shower. That wasn't anywhere close to what they had planned for the beauty wrapped in his arms. He dried her quickly before pulling one of his t-shirts over her head. Christ she was so petite the damned thing hit her below the knees. When she'd tried to put her panties back on he'd shaken his head and stuffed them into one of the pockets of his cargo pants.

"Come on, I'll comb out your hair. Turn around and

stand still for me." She'd given him a wide-eyed stare but slowly turned until she faced the cracked and cloudy mirror over the pedestal sink basin. He made short work of detangling her hair and when he saw the questions in her eyes, he grinned. "It isn't what you think. Sam and I have a couple of sisters and a whole tribe of nieces who love to spend time with us. We learned real fast that bath time was much more peaceful if we knew how to comb out tangles without yanking out handfuls of their hair."

Turning her toward the door, he gave her curvy little ass a swat, "Come on, I'm sure our dinner is probably here by now." He'd pulled his pants back on but hadn't bothered with the shirt, no sense in trying to fool either Carl or Peter. Both were experienced Doms and Sage knew either one of them would have done exactly what he'd done if they'd been given the opportunity. *Not a chance in hell, assholes. This one belongs to us.*

Sam returned to their room carrying several bags of food so they sat Jen between them and dished up. The conversation between the five of them quickly turned to the information the other two hostages had shared with Peter. When he had explained the two women had mentioned Costa Rica, Jen started trembling and her fork had clattered to the floor. She'd looked like every bit of the blood had drained from her face and Sage noticed her breathing had become little more than frantic pants. Placing his hands on either side of her face, Sage forced her to focus on him. "Slow down, Jen. Breathe with me, sweetness. Come on." When her eyes appeared to become even wilder he sharpened his tone, "Stop. Right. Fucking. Now." When she hiccupped a breath he nodded, "Better. Now, match your breaths to mine, baby."

It took several attempts to get her calmed back down

and in the back of his mind, Sage kept wondering what on earth they'd missed. Could she still be reeling in the emotional undertow of what she'd experienced? It didn't seem likely knowing how strong she was. Sure, she'd had a scare in Costa Rica last year but it hadn't been anything that would have prompted a reaction even remotely like what they'd just witnessed. All of them were trained to deal with a variety of possible victim reactions and in his peripheral vision, Sage could see the other three seemed just as baffled by Jen's over the top reaction as he was. Personally, he thought it was much more likely she'd been having some kind of trouble more recently and had failed to mention it to anyone. Thinking about her coping with the kind of threats that would have initiated the reaction they'd just seen had his gut clenching. *Oh, baby, Jax is going to pop a vessel if you haven't kept him apprised of what's happening. And Sam and I are going to set your ass on fire again if that's the case.* Once her breathing appeared to have calmed, he brushed his thumbs over her high cheekbones before speaking to her softly, "Want to tell us what we're missing, sweetness? Because your reaction was totally out of synch with the information we've been given."

Sage watched as her eyes darted to the left before lowering in a classic "I'm going to lie my ass off" move. Hell, the woman was a well-respected expert in the field of body language interpretation so she had to be shaken to her core to make a mistake like that, especially when she was sitting in a room with four Doms, a fact he was sure she hadn't missed. "I don't need to remind you there are serious consequences for lying, sweet cheeks. But I will remind you that editing and omitting facts will have the same consequences as lying. Now, out with it."

When her narrow shoulders sagged in resignation,

Sage knew that at least she planned to tell the truth. He seriously doubted they'd get it all, but he was hopeful she'd spill enough of the beans they'd have some ideas about how to help. Jen took a couple of deep breaths and then started relaying what she had initially considered random events over the past few months. The longer she spoke, the more the hair on the back of Sage's neck stood on end. Sam's wrinkled brow indicated he was experiencing the same concerns. Thankfully whoever had decided Jen Keating was fair game hadn't taken into account the fact she was whip smart and had evidently been born under a lucky star. *Jesus, how on earth has she lucked out so many times?*

Sage made a silent vow to himself that from this point forward she wouldn't be facing the threats alone. Even the luckiest people had to go toe-to-toe with a demon eventually and Sage worried that face-off was coming sooner rather than later. Jen's luck was most likely precariously close to running out.

Chapter Four

LISTENING TO JEN describe what she'd so inadequately described as "the numerous incidents" of the past few months set every warning bell in Sam McCall's head clanging as if they were weathering hurricane force winds. *How does one tiny bundle of gorgeous manage to attract so much trouble? It's absolutely baffling.* The woman was a magnet for trouble and seemed completely oblivious to that fact. Hell, he and his brother were highly trained operatives—among the world's most elite soldiers as a matter of fact, and he didn't doubt for a minute that she'd keep them on their toes for the rest of their lives. *Holy shit! I have to chill out or I'm going to blow this before we've even had a chance to explore it.* Even though they had discussed their hopes that Jen might be the one woman they'd be able to build their future with, Sam knew that plan wasn't even close to being a certainty. Any thoughts to that end were a setup for heartbreak at this point.

Where on earth had his assumption that she would even consider belonging to them forever come from? He and Sage had shared women in scenes for years, but the possibility of them sharing one forever had been little more than a dream before meeting Jen. No one had been surprised when their friends, Kyle and Kent West, settled into a polyamorous relationship because that was how they'd been raised. But Jax McDonald and Micah Drake's recent marriage to Latin beauty, Gracie Santos, had been the first time Sam had seriously entertained the idea that something similar might work out for he and his brother, Sage, as well.

Refocusing his attention on Jen, Sam thought back over various things she'd mentioned happening over the past couple of months. "What was the very first odd thing you remember, doll?"

The disapproving glare she shot him for the pet name made him smile. *Keep it up, little subbie, my palm has been itching to reconnect with your curvy backside for months.* "Honestly, weird shit happens to me all the time so it's hard to say. But the first thing I can remember was the mail in my box being all topsy-turvy." They must have all looked puzzled because she laughed. "The man who delivers mail to my apartment building is absolutely over-the-top OCD. Every piece of mail is *always* facing the same direction and leaning the same way so when I open the box I know I'm going to be able to grab it with one hand." Shrugging at their open-mouth stares, she just waited.

Sage leaned forward and asked the question Sam was willing to bet all four of them were struggling to figure out. "How the hell did you notice this? I mean, really that is a pretty strange observation."

Sam knew Sage hadn't meant to hurt her feelings, but it was glaringly obvious he had. "Well, some of us are just *odd* like that, Sage. I noticed it not long after I moved in, so I hung out in the lobby one day to meet the mail carrier. It turns out he is an older man who takes a lot of pride in what he does. He told me that many of his customers are busy professionals and he knows they are usually carrying laptops, bags, kids, and any number of things when they open their mailboxes. His way of helping them out is to make it easy for them to grab the mail and go. And he is religious about making sure things are just perfect." Sam watched as her cheeks turned pink and he'd be willing to bet she'd befriended the elderly man she obviously respected.

"Jen, I don't think Sage meant any disrespect to you or your mailman. But for guys like us, that kind of observation is so unlikely it's almost funny. We're not as tuned in to that sort of thing unless we're working." Truer words had never been spoken, because that sort of detail wasn't anything he'd have probably ever noticed, let alone recognized so quickly.

Sage leaned back, obviously surprised by Sam's words. "Damn, I wasn't trying to be rude, Jen. But holy fucking cat tracks, noticing that kind of detail really is a testament to how bright you are." He grinned at her and Sam could see some of the tension ease from her posture. "Now, go on— what happened that caught your attention with the mail?"

Jen looked at each of them in turn as if gauging whether or not they were really interested. Evidently satisfied with what she'd seen, she explained, "Well, like I said, I opened my box and everything was messed up. You know, upside down, the front of envelopes facing the back of the stack. Stuff like that, so I asked the security guy at the desk if Tommy was sick. Because Tommy always let me know if he was going to be off work." Her cheeks flamed bright red and she added quietly, "He's a nice man and lonely so I made friends with him. He is supposed to retire in a few weeks and then he's moving to Florida to be near his sister, the lucky dog. I'm planning a little surprise party for him before he leaves though."

Fluttering her hand to the side as if she'd realized how off track she'd gone, she quickly went on. "Anyway, he had

37

been the one to deliver the mail that day, so that told me someone had gone through my mail. It's not like I ever get anything interesting in the mail, but it was still odd and kind of creepy." Odd indeed, and mighty fucking careless of whoever had done it. One of the cardinal rules of Intel gathering was to leave no trace behind, so whoever had gone through Jen's things had either been sloppy or they'd purposely let her know they'd been there.

"Then a few days later I was crossing the street outside my apartment and I was almost run over by a black SUV. If my neighbor, Betty, hadn't waved me over to see the outfit she'd just bought for her new grandson I'd have been the guys new hood ornament. It was the cutest little thing, a sailor sleeper with an anchor on the chest and the little hat, just adorable." Sam looked over at Carl and Peter just as they both covered their laughter with phony fits of coughing. Jen frowned in their direction before shrugging her shoulders. *She has no clue how amazing she is. Her mind works at warp speed on so many different levels simultaneously it has to be utterly exhausting.* CeCe's words rang through his mind with an entirely new level of clarity and truth.

"Everything seemed to be back to normal, or at least *my* normal, for a while..." Watching as Jen pulled her bottom lip between her teeth chewing on it nervously, Sam just waited, letting her work through what she wanted to say. She took a deep breath and then said, "Then...well, I just had this feeling I was being watched. I never could really see anyone out of place, but you know what it's like in D.C. There is craziness and chaos everywhere in that city, so something has to be pretty *out there* to stand out. Anyway, it just gave me the creeps and I started going out less and less. I still traveled for work, but most of those trips have been to much more stable locations than this trip."

Like all good interrogators, Sam knew how to use silence to his advantage so he just waited to see what else she might share. He'd almost decided to call it a night when he noticed her start to fidget in her seat. *Pay dirt.* "And…well, there is the thing with the flowers. That was a little weird."

"Flowers?" Thankfully Peter had asked because Sam had serious doubts about his ability to contain his frustration. *Flowers? Really, Jen? Flowers are the Hallmark greeting of every card-carrying crazy bastard out there, and you mention it last? Almost as an afterthought? Doll, you are racking up so many punishments I'm going to have to start a tally.*

"Well, yeah. At first it was kind of sweet, you know? Like a secret admirer or something. But then the notes started to get a little too personal and…" When she turned to him, Sam realized both of his hands were clenched into fists and he evidently hadn't fully succeeded in suppressing the growl of rage that had rolled through him. *How fucking dare someone threaten her?* Jen stopped talking and Sam wanted to kick himself. *Way to scare our only source of information into silence, McCall.* And the hell of it was he, of all people, should know better. He was the team leader, a highly trained interviewer and negotiator, as well as an experienced Dom. Where the hell had his self-control gone? Had it simply evaporated into steam when his body had enflamed with a need to shield her from harm that was burning from his soul outward until his skin was even starting to tingle? What was it about this woman that flipped every one of his switches? Why did his instincts scream shelter and protect every time he so much as thought about her? *Because she belongs to me and to my brother.*

FUCK, FUCK, FUCKIDY fuck. When will I ever learn to keep my damned runaway mouth closed? Jen could practically feel the anger pouring off Sam and it took everything in her not to cringe away from his touch when he took her much smaller hand in his. She'd known the flowers were going to be a huge issue, but she'd hoped to soften the impact a bit by building up to it. *Yeah right, Fred. That worked out great. Whatcha' gonna do for your next trick, Mensa Girl?* Taking a deep breath, she tried to smile, "Sorry, probably should have led with that, huh?"

This time both McCalls growled at her, but when their buddies laughed out loud Jen couldn't hold back her giggle. Peter leaned forward and patted the back of her hand, "Honey, you are fucking perfect. I'd been dreading this *last* mission with Mr. Large and In Charge over there," he nodded toward Sam, "but you just made it totally worth every bit of melancholy that had surrounded it. But right now, Carl and I are going to do a perimeter sweep and let you guys have some privacy. Then we'll be next door should you need us." When she looked up nervously at them, he leaned down and whispered against her ear, "You got this, girl. No worries."

Sage's snarled, "Out. Get your own woman," made both men laugh out loud again as they gathered their gear and moved to the small hallway. Once they were alone, Jen felt the atmosphere between them switch up like a west Texas wind change before a storm. Looking from Sam to Sage, she noticed their thunderous expressions and knew her storm analogy had probably been all too prophetic.

Since eating seemed preferable to being paddled, Jen

grabbed up a new fork and focused on the very cold plate of food in front of her. Once she'd finished the dinner that had lost its appeal she set her fork down and looked up. Sam simply raised a brow, "Finished, doll?"

"Umm…yes, thanks for asking though." Stretching her arms over her head, she tried to pull up a yawn but her racing pulse seemed to be hell bent on denying her the ruse. "Boy, I'm beat. I think I'll turn in early. Good night, gentlemen."

Just as she started to stand, Sam leaned forward and snapped, "Sit. Down." When she dropped back onto the chair as if someone had cut the strings on a marionette, he nodded once before continuing, "We'll be covering the notes and flowers issue later, doll. Don't think you've gotten away with trying to soften the impact of that particular piece of information with the big round about you took by mentioning everything else first." She must have seemed surprised because she heard Sage's chuckle from her left. "You aren't the only bright person in the room, pet." Jen knew the SEALs were America's best and brightest on a lot of levels so she didn't doubt for a minute what Sam had said was true. "And as it happens we're all very experienced Doms as well. And do you know what that means?" She felt like a deer caught in the blinding beams of oncoming headlights—powerless to look away, and even less capable of fleeing the obvious danger barreling toward her. Fortunately he must not have been expecting an answer to his question because he just continued on, "That means we know when we're being played. In BDSM circles, that stunt you just pulled is known as topping from the bottom."

"And just so you know, sweet cheeks, there isn't a Dom worth his salt that will allow a sub to get away with that kind of behavior. Do you know why?" Sage's words might have sounded soft, but his tone had been laced with an unmistakable steel. This time she managed to shake her head, but he just waited. Their lack of response confused her until she remembered the last time they'd been together they had insisted she use words to answer questions. They had explained verbal responses were required to insure there wouldn't be any misunderstandings between them.

"No, I don't know why. But I'm too tired to worry about it this evening. Perhaps another day? This has been interesting, but I'm exhausted." This time, when she stood, they were on their feet so quickly it startled her.

Sam reached for her wrist and pulled her close enough that she could feel the heat of his body washing over her, setting off tiny sparks of awareness over her skin. "What's your safe word, Jen?" Suddenly her entire body began to tingle in anticipation. *Traitor.* "If you haven't thought up one by now we'll use the same stoplight system we used last time. Tell me what that means so I know you haven't forgotten." She recited the textbook version of the most common safety protocol used in BDSM play as if she were reading it from an invisible book in her head, because that was basically what was happening. She'd done plenty of research into the lifestyle, but knowing and doing were two very different things. When she'd finished he simply nodded before stepping back from her. He crossed his arms over his chest and just watched her for several seconds. She met his eyes and was surprised to see them dilated with arousal. She could feel the flush from her chest was snaking its way up her throat and her heart was beating so wildly she was worried it was going to pound right out of her chest.

LETTING HIS GAZE move slowly over her, Sam was fighting two different battles. First, he needed to ensure he and Sage gave Jen exactly what she needed in this moment. Wild monkey sex was unquestionably one of the best ways he knew to burn off excess adrenaline, but that wasn't what was best for her tonight. The second battle was purely internal. Keeping a lid on his own desire to throw her on to the bed and sink as deep in her sweet heat as he could was going to require a level of control he wasn't sure he had in his arsenal right now.

"Strip." Her eyes had flashed with rebellion so quickly he probably would have missed it if he hadn't been focused solely on her eyes. The woman was trained to read the non-verbal communication of others and that made her keenly aware of her own, and she was damned good at staging it, no denying that fact. But what everyone always seemed to forget was the eyes are the windows to the soul. He'd never understood other Doms' restrictions on letting a sub meet their gaze because there were many ways to mask facial expressions, but the eyes still told the truth— even if it was but for a fraction of a heartbeat. And Jen's blue beauties had just shouted "You want my submission? Earn it." *Well, my lovely pet…game on.*

Chapter Five

SAGE HADN'T MISSED the fire that danced in Jen's eyes when Sam had ordered her to strip, and he knew full well Sam hadn't either. In the future those couple seconds of hesitation before following an order would earn her a few extra swats. But right now, watching her pull his oversized shirt over her head had been well worth the wait. The air conditioning in their room was barely keeping up so he knew the shiver that raced over her ivory exquisiteness wasn't from being cold. The woman standing naked in front of him was as close to physical perfection as Sage had ever seen. Her long blonde hair hung in soft waves down her back, and it seemed to have been woven from a hundred different shades of yellow silk. The dim amber bulbs in the hotel's ancient fixtures highlighting each one of the distinct hues, and he wondered if the gods always conspired to make a woman appear perfect to the men who were destined to fall in love with them.

Hell, maybe she isn't perfect after all. Maybe it's just Mother Nature's way of making sure the species continues. Shaking his head at the insane track his thinking had taken, he looked back at Jen and knew the truth. *Nope, she is abso-fucking-lutely perfect.* Stepping back to let Sam establish his power, Sage picked up his bag and set it on the dresser. He saw her glance his way and then heard her yelp of pain as Sam pinched her pink nipples between his fingers. "Eyes on me, pet. What Master Sage is doing is none of your concern, understand? And from this point forward, the only thing I want to hear from you are answers to direct questions. You are encouraged to use your caution word if you need to, but if we're doing our jobs right we'll know exactly where you are even before your mind has a chance to process all the sensations."

Sam pulled Jen toward the bed and Sage saw a raw power reflected in his brother's eyes that he'd never seen before and knew Sam was falling under her spell too. Sam's words were directed at Sage even though his eyes never left Jen's, "I'm taking a quick shower. Wind her up tight but don't let her come. We'll punish her together when I get out." When Jen let out a quick gasp, Sam used his fingers on her chin to lock her gaze on him. Sage saw her body respond to the intensity Sam was using to make sure her entire focus was on him. "What was that? Using your safe word already, pet? I'd have taken you for being made of stronger stuff than that."

The challenge was a gamble—a huge gamble at that. But Sage knew his brother was one of the most intuitive Doms he'd ever known, so he trusted his judgment. If Sam was willing to throw down the gauntlet, he knew exactly what effect it would have and Jen didn't disappoint. The answering jut of her jaw and narrowed eyes fairly well screamed her intent to meet the challenge head-on. *Yes indeed, the sassy ones are always so much more fun.*

As soon as the door to the small bathroom latched closed she let out a shuddering breath and started muttering to herself. None of it had been intelligible, but that didn't change the fact she was disobeying an order. He gave her a solid swat that immediately had her ass blushing a lovely shade of pink and left a perfect outline of his hand that pleased him more than it probably should have. She started to open her mouth to protest, but snapped it shut. "Wise choice, sweet cheeks. Now come here, I want to touch you." He'd already shed his pants and had to hold back his sigh of satisfaction when he pulled her naked body against his own. Even though she was physically fit, the pillowy softness of her breasts as they pressed against him was a blessed reminder of how much he'd missed holding a woman in his arms. As his chest hair abraded her nipples he felt them draw up into even tighter buds, tempting him almost beyond reason.

Sage had always been more tactile than Sam. When they'd been kids, his mom had always tried to cajole Sam into giving her the same "sugar" Sage gave so willingly. But even though there was only ten months between them, Sam had always embraced his role as the big brother with an over-zealous enthusiasm and he'd viewed hugs as "kids' stuff" from an early age. Sage had teased him hundreds of times about what a fool he was to pass up a chance to feel the softness of a naked woman wrapped in his embrace. In Sage's opinion, there wasn't much in this world that could come close to the intimacy of those moments. And it had always been the intimacy, the moment two souls spoke to one another, that had been what Sage craved.

Once he felt Jen relax in his hold he smiled and kissed the top of her head. "You feel amazing in my arms, sweet cheeks. I can't wait to get your punishment over with so we can play." Giving her a quick squeeze before releasing her, he stepped back and pointed to the bed. "First things first, lay down on your back with your legs dangling over the edge. I want your lovely pussy right at the very edge, baby." Grasping her ankles, he lifted her feet and kissed the tip of each toe before moving her dainty feet so her heels were just barely on the edge of the bed. As he helped her get into position he felt the small quivers of anticipation move through her. She was completely open to his view and the deep pink lips of her swollen labia told him how aroused she was already.

Kneeling down so his nose was just a fraction of an inch from her sweet core, he inhaled the scent that was uniquely Jen. God, the smell of her arousal alone was nearly enough to make him lose his mind. How on earth was he going to taste her and not blow? "Now, you heard Master Sam's order, no coming or you'll just add to the already significant punishment you've managed to earn in a remarkably short amount of time." She didn't answer, but her eyes were as wide as saucers and her quick nod was all he needed since he hadn't actually asked her a question. He leaned forward and licked through her soaking folds, not even trying to hold back his groan of pleasure. The wet flesh was so slick and hot he was fighting off his own need to send her over the top just so he could enjoy the feeling of her coming on his tongue.

It didn't take him long to ramp up her pleasure until he knew she was just a breath away from release, so he pulled back. Her groan of frustration was music to his hears. *Oh, baby, don't think you can steal an orgasm. Pulling one past me is not going to be that simple. Hell, a newbie Dom could have seen that one coming, and by the end of tonight I'm going to know your body even better than you do.*

When she'd settled a bit he pressed his tongue flat against her clit and felt her arousal rocket right back up. Her responses were so perfect, so sweetly wanton that his cock swelled to the point it was almost painful. Swirling the tip of his tongue around the tiny bundle of nerves sticking up so proudly from beneath its hood, Sage smiled when she started panting. Again—just as she was closing in on the point of no return, he pulled back. This time the groan at the loss was more of a growl and he had to bite back his chuckle.

"Your syrup tastes like sunshine and sweet clover, honey. I swear it's more addictive than any drug known to man. I'm not finished making you crazy, baby." This time he ran his tongue deeper into her folds, making several slow, sweeping passes up and then back down just to emphasize his point. When she started to reach for him, he pulled back. "No, sweet cheeks. Put your arms over your head and leave them there or I'll tie you to the fucking bed, do you understand?" He knew she was already sinking into a great state of mind but he wanted to pull her back just a bit and making her answer his question would be just enough to do it.

"Y-yes...yes, Sir." Her stammered reply had been a sweet confirmation that she was right where he wanted her. Obviously she remembered at least some of the protocols they'd instituted with her during their wild night in Austin. The McDonalds had reserved The Driskill's Primrose Suite for Jen and its custom-made bed had been a Dom's dream. The bathroom appeared to have been designed for just the sort of water sports two sexually dominant Navy SEALs would demand even if the entire suite was awash in pink. But truthfully, Jen had been so wound up and just barely sober enough to make informed decisions that it wouldn't have been a huge surprise if she'd forgotten everything. The fact she either remembered or had been studying, pleased him more than just a little.

"I loved the way that sounded, pet." Sage had heard his brother slip back into the room, but from the way Jen stiffened she obviously hadn't. When she tried to sit up,

Sage placed his palm against her lower abdomen holding her in place. Sam watched and Sage could tell he was fighting his own battle to keep from plundering the offering spread out before them. "How does she taste, brother? Is that lush little pussy as sweet and juicy as a peach? Because that is how I remember it was the last time I had the pleasure of burying my face in all that slick sugar."

"It's even better than I remembered, but I have to tell you she has been awfully close to disobeying several times. If I hadn't been paying very close attention our little angel here would have taken her release and never looked back."

"You don't say? Well, perhaps a couple of extra swats might remind her about who is running this show. Hell, I wasn't in the shower long enough that it should have been an issue." Sam waited a few seconds for her to cool down and then stepped closer. "Flip her over. Let's get this done." *Amen, brother. Paddling her ass is going to be a sensual torture for all three of us.*

JEN WAS LOST in a fog of desire so dense that she'd barely registered the fact Sam and Sage had been talking about her as if she hadn't even been in the room. In the back of her mind it registered how much that pissed her off, but with all those lovely little "give it to me now" hormones flooding her brain she couldn't seem to muster enough outrage to complain. But something about being flipped over and her ass displayed over the edge of the bed had shocked her back to the moment. She'd come up fighting when some switch in her mind flipped and the sudden fear that swamped her was all consuming. Nothing existed except escape.

Sam's startled, "What the fuck?" was quickly followed by Sage's inquiry about what the hell had happened, but Jen had crab-crawled to the other side of the bed, kicking off their attempts to grasp her ankles and dropped to the floor before either man could contain her. Blinking up at them as she huddled in the corner, her knees pulled against her chest with her arms wrapped tightly around them. Neither of them moved and neither did she. Her mind was spinning so fast she couldn't get a grasp on any one single thought. The only thing she knew was the myriad of images flashing through her mind were the very ones she'd spent years trying to push back and forget.

No, please! Not tonight, I beg you. She'd spent years learning to block out the memories of the one foster home that had forever changed her. When she'd finally learned to suppress those horrible moments, the panic attacks had slowly faded. Why had she reacted so strongly tonight? One night, one brutal punishment, one man who thought he could control her with violence shouldn't be enough to change her entire life, right? But there were times when it didn't matter how sincere her arguments were, the memory of the absolute terror of that night still won. *But why tonight? Why do I have to freak out in front of the two sexiest men I've ever met? Fatigue?* Or was it the last note she'd received before she'd left D.C.? Just thinking about the pictures and promises her stalker had made sent ice through her veins. *God, a fat lot of good being a Mensa does me when I can't even figure out how to get out of this pickle.* But the one thing she wasn't having a bit of trouble understanding was the two men watching her from the other end of the bed had an intensity that bordered on frightening, and their laser-like focus was not going to be easily dissuaded. She could see the questions in their eyes and this was not a topic she wanted to cover tonight...hell, who was she kidding? She wouldn't ever be ready to answer those questions. *Well, fuck the Fruit Loop fairy, best to just suck it up and plead insanity. Whatever it takes, just don't let them see how scared you are.*

SAM RECOGNIZED THE instant Jen's mind came back to the moment and quickly behind that, the very second she started scrambling for a way to explain her behavior. His own mind was racing with a hundred and one questions about what had just happened, and the only thing he was absolutely certain about was that she was planning to lie to them. Well, perhaps lie wasn't entirely accurate—but she was certainly planning to be selective in what she shared, probably very, very selective. *Give it your best shot, pet.*

Both he and Sage reached into their bags and donned the boxers they pulled out. Once they'd covered their rapidly deflating cocks, Sam walked slowly to the other side of the bed and held out his hand. He was enormously pleased when she didn't hesitate but slid her trembling fingers into the curl of his palm. Wrapping his fingers around hers felt so right, something shifted inside him, and in that instant her fate was sealed. She belonged to them, now they just had to convince her.

Pulling the sheet from the bed, Sam wrapped it around her and picked her up in his arms. He just held her close to his chest and waited as Sage arranged a couple of chairs so once he sat with her on his lap she'd be facing his brother. Even though he knew the time they were taking was giving her a chance to shore up her defenses and bring her story together, Sam also knew he and his brother needed the moment to pull back a bit from the emotion of the moment and get their heads where they needed to be as well.

Sam still fully intended to spank her because that was what they'd told her was going to happen. The one thing he knew above all else was unless they established a solid foundation of trust they'd never truly earn her submission. And God knew the woman was too bright to miss even the smallest inconsistency. So, short of saying her safe word, the shattered sub in his arms would be punished tonight, although he had to admit the dynamics of that had just changed significantly. Since she hadn't reacted negatively until they'd flipped her over on the edge of the bed he could only assume something about that action had triggered her reaction.

As he'd looked in her eyes while she'd shivered in the corner like a frightened animal, the terror he'd seen had squeezed his heart. It had taken every bit of self-control he'd been able to pull together to refrain from pulling her into his arms and coddling her until morning, but somehow he'd known that wasn't what she needed. Hell, he doubted she'd have even allowed it. Sighing to himself, he sat down on the chair and just let her lean against his chest for a couple of minutes. The worried look on Sage's face seemed to have eased a bit, so it was time to find out just what the hell had happened.

Pulling the sheet open enough to expose her pert breasts to their view, he put his hands over hers when she tried to cover herself again. "No, pet, leave it open."

"W-why?" When he didn't respond, she amended her question just as he knew she would. "Why, Sir?"

"Better. Because as you know, the body's responses are

the best lie detectors in the world, and you, sweet sub, are planning to lie for all your worth." He felt her go rigid and wanted to laugh. *Point proven.* "We're going to talk and you are going to answer honestly, do you understand, pet?"

"Yes, I speak English and I'm not a dimwit." *Aha, welcome back, love.* His brother's reaction was so fast Sam doubted Jen had even seen him move until his fingers were pinching her peaked nipples tight enough to make her gasp.

"Watch your tone, baby. You are better than that sort of snark. Now, amend that comment or say your safe word." Sage was often mistaken for a soft touch as a Dom because there wasn't much his brother loved more than holding a woman in his arms. But the truth was Sage was actually more of a stickler for protocol than Sam was, something that most of the subs they'd played with had figured out fairly quickly.

Jen's eyes flamed with an intense heat that let Sam know there was a part of her soul that would only respond to demands for her compliance. She might have a submissive streak that was bone deep, but it was only going to be earned by one or hopefully two men. She wasn't a woman who would ever be able to walk into a BDSM club and willingly submit to any Dom she negotiated a scene with. No, the little bundle of trouble currently pressing her lovely ass against his re-awakening cock would make the Doms in her life earn every inch of her surrender.

Chapter Six

JEN FINALLY MANAGED to squeak, "Yes, Sir. I understand," and Sage released her nipples. Sam knew the little buds were probably throbbing and he hoped it might be distracting enough to keep her off balance just enough that she would answer their questions with more candor. Sam loved having her sitting on his lap for several reasons, but chief among them was the fact he had a front row seat to her sweet sighs and flushing sexiness. Watching her pulse pound at the base of her neck made him want to lean forward and press his tongue flat against her satiny skin and relish her heart's acceleration under his attention.

Jen wouldn't be fooled by false praise, so he simply nodded and said, "Better," when she'd answered more respectfully. He waited a few seconds before starting to give her time to settle and then said, "Tell us what triggered the reaction you had a few moments ago. And the same rules are in place about lying, pet—*always*." Ordinarily he and Sage both insisted subs answer questions without any delay because their answers tended to be much less filtered when they were spontaneous. However, in this case he wasn't sure she really knew the answer so he was going to give her time to work it out. Watching her chew on her bottom lip as she considered the answer was about the sexiest thing he'd ever seen. He didn't doubt she did the same thing when she was deeply immersed in a project or tackling some professional challenge because she'd slipped into thought so naturally. There was the tiniest wrinkle between her brows as she seemed to be focusing all of her energy on processing his question.

Sam didn't get the idea that she was trying to come up with some PCBS answer. Hell, the woman worked for the State Department so politically correct bullshit would be at the top of her skill arsenal in order to survive her day-to-day work environment. The feeling he got from watching her was that she was frustrated with her response to them more than she was confused. Oddly enough he had the impression that she was disappointed in herself for what had happened. *Oh, little over-achiever, getting you out of the whirling mass of thoughts that you're battling is going to bring you a level of peace you have only imagined existed. But teaching you to let go and trust us to take you there is going to be the tricky part.*

He could almost feel the moment she'd formulated an answer to his question and felt more than heard her soft sigh of resignation. *Good, girl. Now, just spit it out.* Her voice didn't shake, but there was definitely a hesitance that he hated hearing as she spoke. "Truthfully I'm not sure it was triggered by any *one* thing...more likely it was a combination of things."

"Sweet cheeks, you can do better than that. Now spit it out. The longer you take to answer, the more difficult it will be to get through." Sage's voice had sounded patient but the sharp edge of frustration threaded through his words wouldn't have been anything the little linguist wiggling on his lap would have missed.

"You're not going to let this go...I get that, but really I'm still trying to work it out myself." Sam could hear the sincerity in her voice and knew they were getting close to the edge of what was no doubt going to be a very blurry line between effective pressure and complete disaster. It was a line he knew they didn't dare cross this early in the game.

Turning her face to his own, Sam spoke softly, "We understand that you've had a lot on your plate, but we also know you're holding back. So tell us what factors you think might have played into what happened and we'll help you sort it through." *Because I have a good idea that you haven't had anyone to talk to for a very long time, if ever, about the problems in your life.* What he did know was that he hoped he and his brother would be able to eliminate that particular challenge for her. "Think about this, pet, what do you have to lose?"

JEN FELT LIKE she was struggling to swim through a pool filled with Jell-O as she tried to focus her thoughts and sift through her memories of what had happened. Her entire life had been defined by bits and pieces for so long that it was often impossible to keep things sorted into any manageable sequence, and to be honest, it was becoming overwhelming even to try. She knew Sam and Sage McCall were good men. Hell, they were amazing men, but they were as much a part of the problem as were part of the solution. It was one thing to talk to a therapist who was a virtual stranger about something that was troubling her. But confiding those same failings to the sexist men she'd ever known was an entirely different matter. *Can you say humiliating?*

Jen had often been accused of turning in on herself when something was troubling her, so she recognized the familiar feelings of detachment that were working their way through her mind. She wanted the familiar numbness that came with shifting everything inward. The power of letting denial swallow her whole was at the pivot center of her ability to project a cool, confident face to the world…a world that rarely took the time to see the desperation lurking behind the outward smiles. She'd been so very close to that escape when she was yanked back to the present by Sam's words, "Think about this, pet, what do you have to lose?" And for the life of her she couldn't come up with a single argument. *Damn.*

Taking a deep breath and squaring her shoulders, she decided he might be right. Maybe they could help her work it out, at the very least they might have some ideas about the stalker she'd acquired. Even Jen knew the behavior of whoever had decided to "possess her body and soul" was escalating. She'd spent a lot of time with her aged grandfather as a small child and one of the things she remembered was him saying "time to fish or cut bait, Jennifer." Sure they'd only been playing kids games, but she'd quickly figured out he was telling her to get on with it…that it was time to act instead of thinking a problem to death.

Straightening her spine, hoping the improvement in her posture would bolster her confidence, Jen nodded once and plunged in. "Okay, I had one experience while I was in foster care that was pretty frightening and painful…and well, that was the position he used." Although the studded belt had been the biggest problem, she thought that might be a bit too much information, considering she'd felt Sam go completely still beneath her. "I was removed from that home the next day when I couldn't sit down at school. In truth it was that incident that brought me to the attention of Millie Sinclair, so it was actually a blessing in disguise.

She changed my life for the better in more ways than I will ever be able to count."

Sage had taken her hand in his and was drawing lazy circles over her palm with his thumb and it surprised her how much that little bit of human contact comforted her. "Add to that the fact I am really strung out after what happened at the embassy...there is just something about the whole thing that doesn't ring true, but I haven't worked it through yet. How many people were there outside? I just have the feeling the whole thing was an inside job."

"WE HAVE THE same concerns, pet, and we've passed that information to our superiors already. There weren't many men securing the facility, which I agree is a huge red flag, but let's let that one sit on the table for a moment. Go on." Sam didn't think she had deliberately veered off the topic; in fact, he'd be willing to bet her thought processes were rarely linear. Thinking back on the lesson CeCe had given them, he made a mental note to send her a big box of her beloved RICHART chocolates. Granted Cam would no doubt snatch them up and dole them out as rewards, but at least she'd know how much they'd benefitted from what she'd taught them that night.

"Oh...okay...sorry, I took a forty-five didn't I?" *Yes, sweetie, you did indeed angle off there for a moment.* He just smiled and nodded. "Well, there is the issues with the pictures, too." Sam froze. He saw Sage's thumb was no longer moving over the baby soft skin of her palm either as they both waited for her to elaborate. Willing himself not to show even the barest hint of a reaction, he just waited—

barely breathing, for her to continue. She must have been satisfied it was safe to go on because she plunged ahead. "I told you about the flowers, but I didn't mention the pictures…well, because it's really kind of gross and more than a little humiliating actually. And I appreciate your teammates and everything, but…" She pulled her lower lip between her teeth and chewed on the delicate skin until he finally reached up and used the pad of his thumb to pull it free. *God, the woman undoes me. And those lips are so fucking kissable and perfect. Sage and I are the only ones who should be nibbling on them.*

"Damn and double damn. I know you're going to rat me out to Jax. And he'll tell Micah. Crap on a cracker, this is going to be a frackster." *Frackster? What the fuck?* She sensed their confusion and giggled. "Sorry. Millie was always getting on my case about cursing, so I started blending things into new words to keep from being scolded. I know she knew exactly what I was saying, but she let me have that little bit of leeway." Sam didn't miss the affection in her voice each time she spoke about the woman she'd lived with and he sent up a silent prayer of thanks that Mrs. Sinclair had been such a wonderful influence.

"Anyway, frackster is code for fracking disaster." He and Sage both laughed because they'd both struggled for years to maintain what their sweet southern mama considered appropriate language for mixed company. His dad's language was still as salty as any man Sam knew, but the fact he was a self-made millionaire many times over seemed to get him a pass with his lovely wife. Their parents hadn't become wealthy until after he and Sage were teens, so he remembered vividly what it was like to work for everything. He'd always been grateful for that because they'd both been well prepared for the hard work it had taken to become a SEAL. Hell, BUD/S had seemed like just another day after the long hours he'd put in helping in his dad's oil fields. Those grueling hours and hard work had been great mental and physical conditioning as well.

"The pictures, pet?"

"Oh, yeah. At first they were pretty lame, you know, silhouettes of lovers holding hands walking along a beach…that sort of thing. Then about six weeks ago they took a really ugly turn." Sam felt her entire body shudder. "I have everything in the little safe in my apartment. And I imaged them also, just in case." *Good girl.* "Also, just in case whoever has decided to 'own me body and soul' decides they don't want the evidence of their little fantasy coming to light. They might get the hard copies, but they'll play hell getting all the imaged copies. I've got several secure on-line backups under different names." *Holy hell, the woman missed her calling, and as they typically did, the powers that be had totally missed her skill-set as well.*

Sage chuckled and leaned forward and kissed her forehead, "I'm impressed, sweet cheeks. And damned proud of you as well. Those back-ups of the images will likely prove very handy." Sam couldn't have agreed more.

"Well, the pictures are pretty graphic and they look like they were taken in a BDSM club. I can tell you they weren't taken at Prairie Winds, but the interior looks a lot like the Wests' club. Unless Ken and Kyle have allowed someone to publish pictures from inside their club, which I'd doubt since I know what sticklers they are about security…well then this club was set up by someone who has been inside Prairie Winds. I haven't actually seen the Prairie Winds club, but I did talk to Jax and Micah about the décor. And…well, I read everything I could about it, too. I was curious…you know?"

Sam was stunned by her words. He didn't question whether or not she was right, because the woman was brilliant and wouldn't have made the connection unless it had been dead on. But the fact someone had visited Prairie Winds and then set up a dangerous imitation was a scary thought. Thinking about whoever had been so incredibly bold that they had actually taken pictures to frighten Jen was downright terrifying. He watched her slip slowly out of the moment, clearly remembering the pictures and no doubt the fear they'd instilled in her. There wasn't anything they could do about that situation tonight, so it was time to change directions. It was glaringly apparent she was folding in on herself, but before exhaustion and stress claimed her, he and his brother needed to show her a few of the benefits of opening herself up to them held in store.

He set her on her feet next to him and ran his fingers softly over her cheek before pushing them gently through the silken blonde tresses. The softness of those pale strands sliding over his calloused fingers was such a contrast he lost his train of thought for just a few seconds. "We are very proud of you, pet. The rest of that story can wait until later. Right now we need to erase those lines of worry from your sweet face. We're still going to give you the swats but I want you over my lap so I can feel all of your softness pillowing against me and warming my cock." What he'd told her was true, even if it was only a small part of it. He wanted to be touching her in any way possible so he could monitor her every reaction and preempt any repeat of what happened earlier.

Sam didn't wait for her to respond, he simply pulled the sheet the rest of the way off and tossed it aside before picking her up and draping her over his lap. Shifting her forward until she was teetering just enough to know he was the only thing keeping her from sliding to the floor, Sam was pleased when she finally relaxed and let him control her position. He ran his hand reverently over her ass, in awe at the perfection of her softly rounded cheeks, he smiled at the look on Sage's face. It wasn't hard to see his brother was as spellbound by the little temptress as he was. Time to get started.

Chapter Seven

SAGE HAD LISTENED closely to Jen's story about everything she'd been dealing with a mix of wonder and rage. Whoever had been harassing Jen was clearly dangerous, and Sage would lay odds the stalker was male. And his escalating behavior was a huge concern. From the little Sage had read about stalking cases, the victims almost always failed to recognize the seriousness of the problem in the beginning, and by the time most of them admitted it was a problem, things were seriously out of control and rarely ended well. He was grateful Jen had people who were willing and more than capable of protecting her, because so many women didn't.

He'd let Sam take the lead because his brother was actually better at controlling his reactions than Sage had ever been. Hell, Sam's poker face was the subject of SEAL legend. Even as a kid Sage had always been more emotionally driven than Sam. And tonight Sage had known Jen needed Sam's unemotional steadfastness while she'd relayed the events of the past few months. But now with her lush ass peaked so perfectly over his brother's lap, all bets were fucking off. There wasn't a chance in hell he'd be holding back on participating in her punishment if it meant getting his hands on her beautiful ass. Jesus, Joseph, and Mary the woman's body was a goddamned work of art. He could see just a bit of tan line and it pleased him that she had obviously chosen a more modest suit. Oh he'd love to see her in a string bikini or better yet nothing at all as she lounged by the pool behind his parents' home, but that bit of visual paradise should be reserved for him and his brother alone.

They had often enjoyed public scenes at the various BDSM clubs they'd visited, but he didn't see them being in any big hurry to display Jen. Sage wondered just briefly about the stab of possessiveness that moved over him, the feeling was foreign, but still felt absolutely right. Sage listened as Sam spoke softly to Jen as he rubbed his hand in slow circles over the ivory globes displayed so beautifully. The first swat had no doubt startled her more than it had stung and Sam's smile confirmed his suspicion. "Four more from me, pet, and then Sage will give you his licks. Since this is your first punishment at our hands, we won't make you count."

Sam's swats to her ass were extremely light-handed considering how his brother usually delivered a punishment, but Sage understood exactly what Sam was thinking. If they pushed her too hard after she'd opened up to them, her mind would link the two events and she'd be reluctant to be forthcoming in the future. It was much better to give her an erotic spanking and let her mind focus on the pleasure it was basking in rather than the fact she was being punished. When Sam's palm landed the final swat, Sage watched him slide his fingers between her legs. The smile that spread over his brother's face told him the little subbie was wet with arousal. *Perfect.*

When Sam removed his fingers, Sage gave him a quick signal telling him to leave her in position. Sage would swat her where she was because he wanted to hurry things along, and standing her up was going to require more time than he wanted to devote to a delay. They were all looking forward to enjoying the rewards to come and as far as he was concerned the sooner he got inside her the better. Sage leaned down and kissed the warm skin that still held the faint impression of his brother's handprint. "Your ass is the loveliest shade of pink, sweetness. It reminds me of the baby blankets our mom makes for all of her friends when they were blessed with little girls." He rubbed his cheek over the heated skin until his brother thumped him on the back of his head jarring him back to the task at hand.

"Get your face away from my crotch and finish this up. I want to feel her wrapped around me a lot more than I want you that close to my junk." Sam's crude words had pulled Jen back just enough and Sage was certain that had been a part of his plan. Sam McCall was a true Master, not only as a sexual Dominant, but he was one of the best strategic planners in all the Teams combined. Sage didn't doubt his leadership skills would be sorely missed by the US Special Forces. Fortunately the men they'd worked with had all either already retired or would be opting out within the next several months. And with the downtime Carl and Peter had coming it was unlikely they'd be sent on another mission unless things blew up on the world stage.

"Ready, baby? Let's get this done so we can show you exactly how much pleasure we can bring you." Sage didn't wait for her reply, instead he let the slaps fall in quick succession. He knew his swats would have stung more than Sam's, but that was exactly what they'd planned. Her yelp at the first blow had changed to a soft moan by the fifth and he wasn't at all surprised to find her soaking wet when he pushed his fingers deep into her channel. Curving them just right, he felt his spongy target and pressed down. "Come for us, baby." Her response was so immediate it had taken both of them to keep her from tumbling off Sam's lap. The gush of cream that washed over his hand felt like warm liquid silk and the smell was pure ambrosia.

By the time they had Jen settled on the bed they'd both shed their boxers and Sage had rolled a condom over his throbbing erection. Her eyes were becoming more focused so it was time to start sending her right back up the steep mountain to release. The difference would be this time he wanted her to take him along on that sweet magic carpet ride over the stars. Moving over her, he kept almost all of his weight off her, only allowing enough pressure that she'd know she was right where he wanted her. "Baby, I'm dying to feel your heavenly body wrapped around my cock. Feeling you clamp down on me is going to be as close to rapture as I'm willing to face at this point in my life. But, sweetness, you are so tight, I need you to relax and let me in."

Even though they'd had a couple of different sexual encounters with Jen, they hadn't ever actually fucked her, and he was stunned at how tight she was. *Holy fucking hell, how long has it been for her? Christ! If I manage to just sink balls deep in her without embarrassing myself I'll count it as a victory.* When the tip of his cock finally made it through the gate he stopped and let both of them adjust. Glancing over at his brother, he groaned, "Fuck me, she is so tight. Like a hot fist with a vise-like grip that is going to make me completely insane." Sage felt sweat bead up on his brow as he fought for control. He pressed his lips against her forehead and whispered, "Baby, you are going to have to relax or this is going to be over long before either of us wants it to." *And that was a monumental understatement if there ever was one.* "Brother, see what you can do to distract our girl, here."

"My pleasure, little brother." Sam moved into position

and held his cock close enough Jen would be able to turn her face and take him into her sweet mouth. "Come on, pet, let's see if we can't get your body to relax a bit by dividing your attention, shall we?" Sage watched Jen's eyes widen and then dilate just before she licked her lips. The groan that came from Sam when her tongue circled the head of his cock before swiping the pearly drop of pre-cum at the end was enough to tell Sage how close his brother was to the edge himself. Hell, Mr. Always in Control wasn't going to last long enough to be any help at all at this rate.

Fortunately the added distraction was having the desired effect and Sage was able to begin painstaking shallow thrusts, gaining fractions of an inch each time, until he could see the flush of arousal spreading over her chest. *Time to ramp things up a bit, sweetness.* Using his knees to spread her legs further apart, he tilted his pelvis and pressed his lips against her ear. "You are ours, love. Never doubt that. Your pleasure, your pain, every worry, is ours to share. So your days of facing problems alone are done."

"Better fast forward, Romeo, because her mouth is either a gift straight from God or the most effective temptation the Devil has ever come up with." Sam's words felt as if he'd thrown gas on Sage's own flame and he started plunging harder and faster, feathering against her cervix with each stroke. And when Sage heard Jen groan around his brother's shaft, he knew Sam was a goner.

Everything seemed to happen at once and Sage knew he'd still be replaying this particular moment in time when he was eighty years old. Sage managed to bite out, "Come for us, baby," just as Sam leaned his head back and shouted as he came, groaning at the intensity of his release. One last thrust had Sage buried so deep he could feel the tip of his cock pressing against her cervix and knew the pulses of his release against her deepest point would send her over. She'd managed to swallow every drop of Sam's essence before she shattered in Sage's arms. As her vaginal walls grasped him with a grip strong enough to make him catch his breath, Sage was bowled over at the continued rippling of her internal muscles as she trembled through several aftershocks that many women would have claimed as a decent orgasm.

Sage was actually damned impressed that his arms held him up considering his entire world had just been completely blown to bits by the woman beneath him. He'd been having sex for the better part of two decades and he'd never experienced anything remotely like what he'd just felt. His dad had taken him aside once just before he'd left for BUD/S and reminded him that there were a lot of women whose heads would be turned by the fact he was a SEAL. Sage had smiled and nodded even as he silently prayed they weren't going to rehash the "keep it wrapped at all times son" or the "don't ever stick it anywhere you'd be ashamed to admit to" speech.

Instead his dad had simply said, "When it's the right woman, everything about it will feel different." Sage was sure his confusion had shown because his dad had slapped him on the back and said, "You'll know it when it happens, son. I just want you to remember this day...and that I warned ya." With that, his dad had hugged him and walked away. He'd often wondered if his dad hadn't just been in a sappy mood that day since he and Sam were both leaving, but now he understood exactly what his dad had been talking about. *Holy fucking hell.*

IT HAD ONLY taken them a few minutes to get cleaned up and Jen settled in the center of the bed. Sage had slipped from the room and Sam could hear him speaking quietly and assumed he was checking in with Carl and Peter. He was also betting Sage would be giving a quick status update to Jax and Micah. Hopefully they could get a leg up on finding the asshole who'd been terrorizing her. Sam knew Jax was going to flip a script that she hadn't called him for help, but Sam also knew enough about working with victims to understand the whole thing had probably gone south slowly enough in the beginning that she kept assuming it was harmless. And by the time it was obvious how far she was in over her head, she was probably embarrassed to have been caught unaware.

Often, when Sam was home on leave, he'd spend time helping in the women's shelter where his mom volunteered, so he'd heard different versions of the tale many times. But even though he'd always felt compassion toward the women, he'd never felt the overwhelming desire to protect them that he felt with Jen. And now, having her ass pressed against him as he wrapped his arms around her, was as close to heaven as Sam thought he'd ever felt. Usually Sage was the one who cuddled the subs they'd shared, but this time Sam had been more than happy to take Sage up on his offer to make the calls.

Sam had whispered sweet words to her and rubbed his hand absently up and down her arm for fewer than five minutes when he heard her breathing even out and he knew she'd fallen asleep. Knowing she felt safe enough in his care to drift off so quickly had his ego inflating along with his cock, which had suddenly noticed how close it was to her very naked sex. Trying to think about anything but the heat coming from her center was like trying to ignore a brass band in the corner of the room. Grateful when his brother returned, Sam looked up and didn't miss the tenderness in Sage's eyes. "God, she is so fucking beautiful." Sam merely nodded at Sage's whispered words because he wouldn't have expected a response to his observation.

"Jax?" Sam asked softly.

Sage shook his head as he dropped his boxers and crawled in bed. "Micah Drake." Sam knew by the grin on his brother's face there was more to hear. "He had the pictures before we even got off the phone. Evidently he already had one of sweet cheeks on-line backups tagged so it was a snap for him to pull it up. To say he was pissed would be a huge understatement. I'd say our little subbie is going to get it with both barrels when he and Jax get a hold of her."

Sam didn't even want to think about the content of the pictures. Hell, just that fleeting thought sent his blood pressure up. Sighing to himself, he decided if he had any hope of enjoying his "retirement" he needed to learn to live in the moment, and that meant spending quality time with the people in his life. He leaned down so his nose was pressed against Jen's hair and just breathed her in before kissing the top of her head. Opening his arms, Sam let Sage pull the sleeping and pliant women into his arms. He smiled at her sleep grumbling, and watched Sage move his hands up and down the full length of her spine in a soothing gesture that was so typical of his younger brother.

The McCall brothers were sought after Masters in various clubs they'd visited all over the world because of the skills they brought to any scene they participated in. Subs bragged about the fact their methods never failed to send them into the sweet abyss of sub-space, but almost without fail they also commented on the tenderness and intimacy of Sage's after-care. Sam had never participated in that part of their interactions with submissives, and had never considered that he'd missed anything of significance until now. Holding Jen Keating after a sexual release that had probably pinged local Richter scales, Sam had felt their souls connect most during those quiet moments when she was nestled safely in his embrace. *Amazing!*

Chapter Eight

JEN HAD BEEN on a slow simmer, which was fast approaching a rolling boil, for the past half hour. Jax had been avoiding her for several days and now that she'd finally managed to get he, Micah, and the Wests all in one place they were dancing on her last nerve by lecturing her. *As fucking if. This whole Jen is a naughty girl speech might have worked out a lot better if they hadn't let her get her bearings over the past few days. Asshats.* By the time they'd made their way back from Bolivia she'd endured hours of travel time in a variety of vehicles, several of which had been of questionable origin, and she'd been completely spent.

By the time Sam and Sage McCall had let her off at the West's front door she'd barely been able to hold herself in the seat of the cart Tobi had used to drive her down to the guest cottage. She'd stumbled inside, barely managing to make it to the bedroom, before she'd collapsed on to it and fallen into the sleep of the dead. She'd slept for sixteen hours straight, and when she'd finally managed to stagger back to Prairie Winds main building, tornado Tobi had swept her up and hadn't let up until Jen had finally begged for mercy. How the woman could spend so much time shopping for absolutely nothing was a mystery to Jen. Each day Jax and Micah managed to avoid her had eroded her patience and sent her frustration with the entire situation so high that she'd almost been able to feel it vibrating through her. She was getting fewer hours of sleep now than she'd gotten in months and the four hours of tossing and turning she'd endured last night hadn't been even close to enough for her to get her through this meeting.

Sitting in Kent and Kyle West's office listening to four former SEALs berate her as if she were a learning challenged third grader was just fucking annoying, there wasn't any other way to view it. *Well at least Sam and Sage McCall aren't here to add their two cents.* The fact they'd all but left her at the front gate of the Masters of the Prairie Winds Club that first night still chafed her ass. They'd blathered on about having to return to the Seal Cave—or wherever SEALs go after their missions—but it still frosted her cookies. *Talk about feeling like a stray kitten. Yep…I could almost hear them telling Jax, "Here's your bratty little sister. Rots a ruck, buddy."* They hadn't even called her and that stung more that it should have. *Geez, pathetic much?* The only people who hadn't raked her over the coals today were Gracie and Tobi. They'd both been wonderful and had even tried to interrupt the inquisition several times to no avail. *Gotta give the Doms credit, they're a focused lot that's for sure.* But in all her erotic romance novels the Doms were focused on the reactions of the submissive almost to the point where they seemed to read their minds. Well, that was obviously not the case here, because if these four could read her mind they'd be none too pleased with her.

Just a few moments ago, Gracie had turned a lovely shade of lime green and run from the room with her hand plastered over her mouth. *Nope, doesn't take a medical degree to figure that one out.* Tobi had been on Gracie's heels so now Jen sat listening to the third verse of "why you should have called us as soon as this all started" without any moral support. She fought against the urge to roll her eyes, the only thing missing was a nice hallelujah chorus after every stanza. And the part that frustrated her the most was that she'd actually tried to call Jax from the airport before she'd left Washington but hadn't gotten an answer. When she'd pointed that fact out to him, he'd reminded her that she hadn't left a message either. *I can just imagine how that would have gone over.* He'd have pulled strings all the way to the top and had her yanked back from an important job assignment without ever batting an eye.

Jen knew her control was beginning to fade. She hated feeling out of control because she either became a raving lunatic or she cried, and she *really* hated to cry. *So...raving lunatic it is.* Standing quickly, Jen spread her feet apart, fisted her hands on her hips, and began tapping her foot. "Listen to me you four overbearing asshats. I'm done with this. Got it? You have played the same tune for an hour and a half, hell, Helen Keller would have heard the damned message by now. When someone is interested in discussing solutions rather than scolding me about something I can't change, feel free to look me up. In the meantime...I'm heading back to Washington. I have a job and I need to report to my superiors. You have stalled me for days. You even sent me to a doctor I didn't need to see. Having a shrink meet us for lunch to assess me." She rolled her eyes at their surprised looks. "Seriously? You didn't think I'd know? You guys suck at this super spy shit, no wonder you need to blow up stuff."

By this point she was on a roll and had started pacing the length of the room. If she didn't work through the energy quickly, she'd wear a path in front of the floor to ceiling windows looking out over the small lake along their fence-lined driveway. Oh the club was a stunning piece of real estate there was no question about that. But Jen wasn't dim enough to miss the fact she was basically a prisoner and she was tired of playing defense. "I need to get back to Washington. I have a career and even though I'm sure you've let the department know where I am, that doesn't mean I don't need to get back to work." She had already scheduled a long break before she'd left for La Paz, but she wasn't going to tell them that. *Jerks*. The truth was she would prefer to be in Texas because returning to Washington where her stalker was no doubt awaiting her return didn't hold any real appeal. However, they'd pushed her into a corner and she'd come out fighting, even when winning wasn't what she really wanted.

"It's easy for you to sit here and pick apart my decisions, because hindsight is twenty-twenty. But my life has always been filled with nonsense and chaos, so subtle changes aren't always that easy to discern. And then by the time it was obvious things were FUBAR—and yes I know that's SEAL-speak for fucked up beyond all recognition—anyway, things were already such a disaster and I didn't think they were likely to get worse while I wasn't available for Stanley Stalker. And I had to prepare quickly for a trip that seemed to crop up out of nowhere." Taking a couple of deep breaths and muttering to herself about the manifestation of the God complex in the Y-chromosome, before she finally turned and asked, "Does it occur to you that *this*," sweeping her hand between the four of them, "overreaction might have been part of my hesitance to involve you?"

She returned to pacing because if she didn't expend some of the energy the top of her head was going to blow off. "I love Tobi, but I know a capture, distract, and detain ploy when I see one. And by the way, once I figured out you were using shopping as a way to keep me busy, I encouraged my shop 'til you drop pal to buy every single thing in sight." She gave them an evil smile before adding, "It cost you...plenty." Both Kent and Kyle groaned, which even Jen knew was for show because the men were loaded. The money Tobi had spent would have been like Jen buying a pack of gum.

"I don't have a phone, my purse is gone so I've got to call my bank and all my credit card companies. I have to get another laptop and replace all my IDs. Crap, I have to get my passport replaced, too. I'm going to wring Ambassador Weasel's skinny neck if this was a set-up. The whole thing stinks to high heaven if you ask me." She'd finally run out of steam and just stood staring out the window for several seconds. "Hell, I don't even know for sure why you are keeping me. The night the McCall brothers brought me here I felt like a stray cat that someone wanted to drown in the river, but didn't even care enough about to make the trip to the bridge...so they just drop kicked me out at the curb instead." She sighed and shook her head, "Damn, you'd think I'd be used to that sort of thing, but as it turns out—not so much." She hadn't actually intended to say the last words out loud, but it was too late...no way to pull them back now. Turning away from the windows to face the room, she froze. Everything and everyone faded into the background as her attention focused solely on Sam and Sage McCall leaning against the doorframe in mirrored poses that looked deceptively casual. Instinctively Jen knew better. She recognized a predator's stance when she saw it.

Her mind was reeling with what she'd just revealed and she wanted to curse her loose tongue. *Way to sound needy, Jen.* Not intending to let them get the upper hand, Jen looked at them and then did her best to pretend their sudden presence in the room hadn't stolen the wind from her sails. Turning to Jax she asked, "Will you help me get a phone and arrange transportation back to D.C.? I'll pay you back as soon as I get access to my bank account. I'd like to leave as soon as possible." Then she turned to Kyle and Kent West who were obviously trying to hold back their responses. "I want to thank you for your hospitality. I appreciate you pinch hitting for Jax and Micah. I know they have their hands full with Gracie not feeling well and that is exactly as it should be. But it is time for me to return to reality and for me...that is in Washington."

Jen wanted to scream because now there were six men staring at her as if she'd sprouted horns and was speaking in tongues. *What is it with Doms, anyway? If you don't say what they want to hear, they just pretend like they don't understand you. It's lame. Well guess what, fellas, that intimidate-with-silence routine of yours isn't going to work on me.* One of her foster fathers had used the same trick, although Jen would have considered his bullying because he recruited others in the house to "ice-out" the victim as well, so she'd become immune to that particular manipulation a long time ago.

Fortunately, Jen had watched when Gracie had left earlier and knew there was another exit from the room even though it wasn't obvious. Exuding a sense of confidence she wasn't really feeling, Jen turned and headed for the door. Just as her hand settled on the handle, she heard Jax's growl of frustration at the same time Sam McCall barked, "Stop." *Seriously? He thinks he can drop me off like a bag of dry cleaning and then waltz back in barking commands and I'll just obey like a trained hound? Well think again mister.*

Chapter Nine

SAM McCALL WAS seeing red and the chuckles from his friends and former teammates weren't helping ease the situation at all. The problem was, he wasn't entirely sure who he was more frustrated with, the sprite with the battered heart who'd just stalked from the room wearing her warrior's heart on her sleeve, or himself. He and Sage had stepped into the room just as Jen had started her tirade, and had watched it play out in amusement. Sam had been keeping track of all the punishment swats she was racking up, and enjoying the hell out of her quick wit and keen intelligence since it hadn't been directed toward him. But when she'd spoken about them "dumping her off" on the Wests and how she should be used to that by now, his heart had been torn in two by the unmistakable pain in her voice.

It hadn't occurred to him she would view their quick exit as abandonment, but now that he considered it—her response was probably reasonable for someone without any real experience dealing with the end of mission protocols the military values so highly. They'd needed to get back to the airport quickly to make the turnaround flight to Coronado. Their debriefing had taken longer than they'd anticipated but the pay-off had been that they were now officially on leave until their separation date in three weeks.

He and Sage hadn't wasted any time packing up what little personal belongings they kept in their apartment, loaded their trucks, and had driven straight through. He'd been wired since they'd hit the state line and each mile closer to Jen had added fuel to the fire burning in his gut. The bottom line was he'd been so focused on tasks that he'd forgotten the feelings of the woman they were racing to rejoin. Hell, she hadn't been out of his thoughts for more than a few hours at a time since they'd met her. The woman was fast becoming an addiction.

She'd turned and the beautiful eyes that were usually such a sparkling crystal blue were darkened with the turbulence of a churning sea. Their gazes had locked for just a few seconds, but it had been long enough that he'd seen how much she regretted the depth of emotion she'd just revealed. Though a part of him was pleased to have witnessed such a candid moment, a much larger part of him was deeply ashamed of the fact he and Sage had put the sadness in her expression. Jen had clearly felt abandoned when they'd left her at the club and he wasn't sure why that surprised him. Pushing his fingers through his hair in frustration, he'd known she'd slept through most of the arrangements they'd made that night, so she hadn't heard all the care they'd taken to be sure she'd be protected until they returned. And their lack of contact the past few days had only reinforced the feeling she'd been handed off like a baton in a relay.

When she'd only hesitated briefly when he'd told her to stop, he'd known they had their work cut out for them. Walking away hadn't been what her heart had wanted to do, but it had been what she thought was best for her. Her trust was shattered and winning it back was going to be an uphill battle. Sam wanted to kick himself for how inconsiderate they'd been of her feelings. *Fuck! I've become so accustomed to working with men whose lives often depended on following my orders I've forgotten how to make a woman see what she might gain by obeying. I've broken one of the fundamental rules of BDSM—hell of all relationships, to make sure your partner feels cherished.* The quiet snick of the door as it closed behind her had sounded like a cannon in the quiet room. Turning his attention to Jax McDonald, he snarled, "You didn't tell her, did you?"

"Fuck you, skippy, this isn't sixth grade and I'm not responsible for passing your notes to the pretty girl in the front row. Hell, I warned you this would happen." When Sam and Sage both straightened from their positions against the door's oak frame Jax waved them off. "Yeah, I told her—mostly. But she wasn't interested in my, what did she call it?" he looked over at Micah and grinned, obviously enjoying his and Sage's predicament. "Oh yeah, now I remember. She explained in clear and concise terms that she wasn't interested in second-hand excuses from my boulder noggin' buddies." The ass had the nerve to pause for dramatic effect before continuing, "And she thought it necessary to explain there wasn't any reason a free-spirited woman couldn't enjoy the mattress mambo with a couple of *players* without needing to touch base with them again. And I believe the phrase 'no harm-no foul' was in there somewhere too, but truthfully by that point I was trying to tune her out because that was too much information from the woman I consider a second sister."

He heard his brother groan beside him as Sam buried his face in his hands. It must have been all it took to break the tension in the room because all four of their former teammates burst out laughing. Jax shook his head and motioned them into the room. "Jesus, McCall, you're too easy. And yes, I gave her the message. But the rest of it was true as well and honestly, we've stalled her about as long as we dare."

Micah stepped forward and shook their hands, "Glad to have you guys here. But I think you did Jen a huge disservice by not calling her. Might want to give those courting skills a dust-off, guys."

Jax's entire demeanor seemed to shift as his eyes narrowed, "About that. While we're on this topic let me just put it out there and explain this as clearly as I can—hurt her and you'll deal with me."

"And then me," Micah added.

"Oh for the love of all things holy, the testosterone level in this room is going to peel the paint off the walls and melt the paint off those lovely Remington oils my husbands value so highly." Tobi West had entered the office and stood with her arms crossed over her chest like a disapproving schoolmarm. Well, as much as a petite, totally stacked blonde beauty could play the role anyway. Sam and Sage had both been completely charmed by their friends' new bride when they'd met her at Jax and Micah's wedding to Gracie seven months earlier. It had been abundantly clear how smitten Kyle and Kent West were and why.

Tobi was obviously whip smart and her irreverent way of humbling her Dominant husbands seemed to endear her to everyone she came into contact with. From what Sam had seen, Tobi was as kind and as genuine as they came— and those traits were what made women beautiful in Sam's view. It didn't matter how lovely the wrapping, if a woman only saw what was in a mirror, she didn't hold any appeal for him. Smiling to himself, Sam thought back on a conversation he'd had with Tobi early on the morning of the wedding. He'd seen her hovered over a table by the pool just before dawn and had gone outside to investigate.

What he'd found had floored him. Hell, she'd married into one of the wealthiest families in the state but she was super-gluing her flip-flops back together and muttering about how you couldn't buy anything that lasted anymore. When he'd inquired why she didn't simply replace them, she'd shrugged and said, "I paid seven dollars for these, damn it. They should last more than two years." When he'd chuckled her cheeks had flushed bright pink. The irony that most of the women who ran in the social circles that could afford the steep membership fees of the Prairie Winds Club wouldn't wear a seven dollar pair of shoes to take out the trash, let alone wear them for more than one season hadn't been lost on him.

When Tobi started tapping her foot in the same impatient way he'd seen his mother use with his dad, Sam's attention returned to the present and he realized she was staring at him with her head tilted to the side as if she were trying to decide whether or not he was listening to her. *Umm, that would be a big no, darlin'.* "You didn't hear a word I said, did you? Good Lord, you aren't going to be another wall of human flesh that I talk to are you? Because really, I'm pretty well covered on that front. After you helped me with my...umm, little project," he watched her eyes dart guiltily between her husbands before she went on, "and you didn't make fun of me, I thought maybe you were different." *Yep, feeling like a major ass now.*

"Project, kitten?" Kyle's voice was curious, but his question was more of a command for her to be forthcoming than just an inquiry.

Sam saw her start to roll her eyes and wanted to smile when she caught herself. *Good save, sweetie.* "Drown me."

Sam saw the corner of Kent's lips curve up despite the fact he was trying like hell to fight the smile. "I was fixing my flip-flips the morning before the wedding and Sam helped me." Waving her hand she said, "I know, I know, I'm not supposed to do that, but damn it those were expensive and they should last longer than that."

Kent hadn't been able to hold in his snort of laughter and even Kyle was grinning as he spoke to Tobi. "Kitten, the reason we don't let you use the super glue is because you glued your fingers to the table—twice, not because we're opposed to you fixing something. Although I do have to wonder why you didn't simply buy another pair of shoes. And we'll be chatting about your disobedience later, my love."

"In the meantime, tell Sam and Sage what you have to say without the snark. They are still friends and Masters who deserve your respect."

Kent's words obviously surprised her and her eyes jerked back to Sam's. She looked at Sage as well before nodding and returning her attention to Sam. "I didn't mean to be rude, but I'd gotten the impression when we first met that you were men who knew the value of a woman's trust. When you didn't make fun of me or run off tattling, I assumed….well, never mind that. Let's just say I expected more from you." Her posture softened a bit as she continued, "I've spent the past few days trying very hard to distract Jen from becoming a rolly-polly bug."

Sam felt his brows knit together in confusion and Tobi didn't miss it. "You know, those little black bugs that curl into a tight little ball when you touch them? Well, anyway that is what she wanted to do. Curl into a ball and protect herself…use that hard outer shell to defect the danger of being touched by someone that was ultimately going to hurt her." Sam could see the unshed tears in her eyes and felt like an ass for involving her in their mess. "You can't be inconsistent with someone who has experienced aban-donment, guys. It is just too painful." Kent and Kyle flanked her and it was clear she felt grounded by their touch. "But I really came to let Jax and Micah know that Gracie really is feeling punk, I'm worried she is becoming dehydrated. And to let you know Jen has called a cab and plans to leave within the hour."

For a few seconds no one moved. Tobi had swung a baseball bat in a room filled with the finest crystal and she'd done it with such finesse they'd all been blindsided. *Holy hell that woman is a force to be reckoned with.* As the room erupted into a flurry of activity Sam saw Kyle pull Tobi into his arms and kiss her soundly before turning her into his brother's waiting arms. *That is what I want with Sage and Jen, because heaven knows it is going to take both of us to keep up with her.*

Chapter Ten

SAGE WALKED BESIDE Jen as she stalked through the arrivals corridor at Dulles marveling at how she could walk so fast on a slick marble floor in spikey heels and not bust her ass. *Incredible.* Once they'd shut down her hastily assembled plans to travel alone to Washington, the security team had put together a safer plan and made the arrangements easily. Sage was convinced the only reason she'd agreed to wait was that Jax had refused to get her an ID and she'd known she couldn't board a commercial flight without one. Of course, the hour-long chat Bill and Carol McDonald had with her behind closed doors had seemed to cool her temper considerably as well. A true Southern belle, Carol McDonald was fire wrapped in pure class. God he loved southern women. They could smile and "honey-pie" you even as they lit the fuse that would launch your ass right off their planet. He could just see Carol brushing her hands together saying "See there? Problem solved" as whoever had annoyed her was rocketed into oblivion.

The plane ride had been frosty, hell, Sage hadn't seen a ray of warmth from her since that first "lock-on" in the West's office. Oh, her eyes had given her away completely in a moment so brief Sage might have missed it if he hadn't been totally focused on her, but the longing and desire he's seen had been shoved deep ever since. Once they'd worked out a plan to accompany her back to Washington, Jax and

Kyle had drawn the short straws to tell her. They'd watched from the safety of the control room as she'd lobbed argument after argument at both men before storming out of the room spitting like a pissed off kitten.

Micah had chuckled and said, "Well, that went well. Anybody interested in taking bets on how long it takes for our phones to start ringing?" The words had no sooner left his friend's mouth than Kent's phone started playing, Kenny Chesney's "You Had Me From Hello". There hadn't been any question who was calling when he'd visibly cringed before cursing Micah for jinxing him. Kent had been vindicated when Micah's phone had started playing The Starland Vocal Band's "Afternoon Delight" in less than a minute.

Since the only bag they'd checked was the one with their weapons, their stop at the security center had been their only delay in leaving the mayhem known as Dulles International. It had only taken them a half hour to make their way to long-term parking where Jen had left her car. And in truth, calling it a car was a generous over-exaggeration. Both he and Sam were six foot three and when they stood staring at her Mini Cooper, Sage saw Jen smile for the first time in two days. "Feel free to rent your own vehicle, gentlemen." With that she unlocked the door, got in and started the motor leaving them to scramble into the sardine can with her. Sage now understood why his dad had been so adamantly against his mom buying a sports car. Jesus, Joseph, and Mary the tiny tin can he was riding in couldn't possibly protect the driver or passengers from serious injuries. *Christ, it's a skateboard with a tin can tacked on top.* As soon as they got her back to Texas they'd see about getting her something suitably safe to drive. Giving himself a mental head slap, he thought, *maybe you should concentrate on just getting her to talk to you first before you try to dictate what she can drive, McCall.*

Sage had dealt with Jen's silent treatment for about as long as he intended to. Sure, he understood why she was frustrated. And he was willing to concede that maybe Tobi and Gracie were right, they'd had their heads up their asses. Damn, even Mama McCall had ripped them a new one when they'd Skyped with her last night. But really, how long could she stay mad? *Why can't women be more like men? We pound the shit out of each other and then it's over.*

As they walked into the lobby of her apartment building, he saw Jen visibly tense. Sage immediately stepped in front of her and stopped her progress, "What's wrong?"

To her credit she didn't brush off his question, and the worry was easy to see in her beautiful blue eyes. "I don't know, really. There is just something amiss. The hair is standing up on the back of my neck and I've learned ignoring those signals never works out well for me." When she opened her mailbox Sage heard her gasp. Looking over her shoulder, he could see the contents of the box were a jumbled mess.

Jen turned toward the man standing behind the reception desk, and extended her hand, "Hi, I'm Jen Keating, where is Matthew?" The guy didn't look like he could be a day over eighteen and suddenly Sage felt every one of his thirty-four years. *Jesus, was I ever that young and naïve? And if he doesn't stop looking at our woman like she is some snack for him to taste he's not going to live to be old enough to buy his own damned booze.*

"He got stabbed. Right here in the lobby. I got called in from the agency to pinch-hit and I told them I wanted hazard pay, ya know? Guess the old goat wouldn't answer some prick's questions so the guy stuck him." Sage stepped up and wrapped an arm around Jen when she swayed on her feet. He wanted to punch the kid for his insensitivity. *Yeah, great example of do as I say, not as I do, McCall.*

"And Tommy?" When the kid didn't seem to understand her question, she added, "Our regular mail carrier? I can tell he wasn't the one to put the mail in my box."

"Oh yeah, guess he bailed early. That's what one of the old ladies upstairs said. The day after the old guy was stabbed here in the lobby, the mailman got roughed up outside so he moved. People said something about some lady named Jen planning a party." NASA's missing rocket scientist looked like a light bulb had just lit up over his head, "Hey! Are you the Jen that was doing the party?" Sage had to hold back his laughter when he heard Sam growl behind them.

Sam stepped around them and asked Einstein, Jr., "Where are the security feeds for the lobby and street cameras stored? Did the police take them? Are they off-site or recorded here?" The kid looked confused and unfortunately he seemed to be suddenly getting a clue that he was talking too much. Sam hadn't even given him time to answer when he turned to Jen, "Do you have a weapon in your car by any chance?"

"No, my pistol is in the safe upstairs." Sage hated the way her voice was shaking, but glad she was aware what they were hearing was probably not a series of unrelated events. He and Sam pulled their weapons out as they took the elevator to her floor. Since they wouldn't leave her in the lobby unarmed, she was between them as they stepped off the elevator and made their way down the hall. They had nearly made it to her door when they were greeted by a woman whose beehive hairdo added a full foot to her four foot height. She was wearing a shocking pink jogging suit and carrying a small dog that looked like something out of a Saturday morning cartoon.

"Jen, darling. I'm so glad to see you are finally home. Things have just gone to hell in a hand basket here, dear. Matthew was stabbed right there in the lobby, he's still in the hospital but expected to make a full recovery. I signed your name to the card, honey, so don't you worry about that. Oh, and did that dweeb downstairs tell you about Tommy?" *Dweeb? Holy shit, where did an eighty-year-old woman learn that term?*

"Yes, Betty, he mentioned that. Can you tell me anymore about it?" Jen had hugged the woman and was absently scratching the dog's ears. It was obvious they were well acquainted and Sage found himself grateful she'd had people in her life that seemed to care for her. It was easy to see Jen was one of those people that others naturally gravitated toward and he'd found it interesting to watch how she charmed everyone she encountered. Hell, even the surly checker in the airport's snack stand had smiled and wished her a good day before growling at the next customer.

"Well, it started the day after you left. That was the same day my son sent me the pictures of Brandon in that little sailor outfit. You remember? I showed you that little blue number out on the street the day the big SUV nearly hit you." She turned to Sage as if to explain, "Drivers in D.C. are insane. They think if they are driving a big truck with tinted windows they are clandestine. Wannabes is what my Herb always called them. Did I tell you my husband was a Marine? Oh, yes, he was a real hottie in his day."

Sage was starting to get dizzy trying to track the conversation but when he looked at Jen, she was patiently ruffling the pooch's ears and smiling. "Well, anyway, first Matthew was stabbed, and then Tommy was assaulted outside. He was really shaken up. I saw him before the ambulance took him. He just kept saying that he didn't know where you were, but the guy wouldn't believe him. Then there was your cousin, my those scars are awful. Was he is some kind of a fire?"

Jen had gone completely still. "Cousin? Fire?"

Betty looked aghast and then started shaking her head. "Damn. I thought it was odd that you hadn't called me. After all, I could have packed up things for you and sent them. Men just don't pack like women do, they forget the important things sometimes. I met him in the hall and he said you'd had a death in the family...bet that wasn't the truth either, was it?" She didn't wait for an answer before plunging ahead. "The lying dirt bag said he was getting a few things together for you. I didn't tell him I had a key or offer to let him in because, well to be perfectly honest, those scars are a bit off-putting if you know what I mean. He seemed distant, but pleasant, and although it seemed weird...this is Washington D.C. and the whole damn city runs on weird. Fiddle faddle, honey, I'm sorry. I should have called the police and let them sort it out, but some-times I'm not as sharp as I used to be."

Jen patted the older woman's hand and Sage saw how her fingers trembled. "Jen, how about you let Sam and I check out the place first while you wait with Ms. Betty?" He gave the older woman what he hoped was a warm smile that she returned, but Jen didn't seem inclined to take his suggestion.

"Well, thanks so much for your kind offer, Sage, but the best you're getting from me is to let you two warriors enter first since you're the ones with weapons." The overly saccharine tone she'd used told Sage that she wasn't over her "mad" yet, but at least she was speaking to them now.

"Oh, honey, if you want a gun, I can help you out." And with that Betty pulled a Dirty Harry special from the tote bag draped over her arm. *Holy shit Sherlock, how had he missed that kind of weight in her bag? Christ Almighty, that kind of mistake in the field could easily cost a soldier his or her life.* Guerilla Granny's laughter cut through his thoughts just as he heard Sam's muttered curses behind him. "Oh, sonny, you are a hoot. You should have seen the look on your handsome face. Let that be a lesson to you. Don't turn your back on anybody in this town, not even sweet innocent looking little old ladies." He and Sam both nodded numbly.

"Well, perhaps you could tell these two Navy SEALs what you did before you retired, Betty." Jen was already moving down the hall with her key in her hand so Sam trailed her while Sage looked down at Betty.

The white haired woman giggled again before leaning in to whisper, "I was a spook. Worked for the CIA until about ten years ago. Truthfully it got easier after I got older because no one suspected me." She batted her eyes at him and he had to chuckle. "Now, you go on and see what kind of a disaster scar face left in there and I'll start writing down things for the detectives I know your brother just called."

Chapter Eleven

JEN HANDED SAM her key and when his fingers brushed hers the arc of electricity that surged up her arm caused her to suck in a quick breath. Damn her traitorous body. Why didn't it listen to her head, which had been broadcasting warnings as loud and clear as those annoying Emergency Broadcast tests on television? She'd managed to stay mad at them until they'd all walked up to her car. Seeing the incredulous looks on their faces had nearly had her howling with laughter. The only other person who'd given her that look about her car had been Jax, and he hadn't even attempted to fold his six foot eleven inch frame into the small car the last time he'd visited her.

Thinking back on their conversation with Betty, Jen knew her elderly friend had been slipping a bit lately or she'd have never let a stranger into her apartment. Jen made a mental note to call Betty's son to make sure he was checking on his mom regularly. Since she was going to be returning to Texas for a couple of weeks, Jen wanted to make sure he knew his backup wasn't going to be available. Ben Remly was a nice guy, but his socialite wife and new baby kept him busy enough that checking on his mom sometimes fell by the wayside. The minute Sam opened the door the smell of stale perfume hit her like a rolling wall of stench.

Sam had pulled the gun from where he'd nestled it in

the back waistband of his jeans and held it low but at the ready. He asked her to stay in the small foyer while he and Sage cleared the small apartment and she agreed. Even from her position by the door she could see the place had been ransacked. She watched as they used hand signals to communicate and taking only a few short minutes to determine no one was inside. Sam was already talking on the phone when they returned to her. It wasn't until Sage pulled her into his arms that she realized she was shaking like a leaf.

"I'm sorry, baby. The place has been wrecked. I'm not sure what he was looking for, but he didn't leave a single thing undisturbed. We won't touch anything because this is a crime scene and even though I doubt seriously there is any valuable evidence, we won't take a chance on destroying something that might help us find out who did this.

"I want to see," was all she managed to stutter and she was grateful when he didn't argue.

"Okay, we'll walk through. But I want you to be really careful where you step and don't touch anything, got it? Also, keep a look out for anything that isn't yours, okay? Anything he might have left behind will be something we want to point out to the lab guys."

The next several hours passed in a blur. Jen was amazed at the violent and personal nature of the destruction. Whoever had done this wasn't just looking for something. No, this was an act of anger and the perpetrator had been sending her a very clear, very personal message. Someone intended to frighten her and they'd succeeded. But the single piece among all the shattered fragments that had once been her life that sent ice through her veins was the note scrawled across Elza McDonald's picture. *Your friend will pay for your misdeeds.* When Jen had read the words, black spots started dancing in her vision. She'd heard Sam shouting her name, felt Sage pull her against his chest, and then everything had gone black.

JAX MCDONALD HAD been fielding calls since Jen and the McCalls entered her building, and each call had heightened his concern. But *this* call sent terror through every cell of his body. Jax had been on SEAL teams that stormed full speed ahead into every imaginable danger and he'd never so much as flinched. However, Sam McCall's words had leveled him. Snapping from the daze, Jax realized that Kyle was shouting at him to sit the fuck down. Numbly Jax complied, falling onto the bar stool he'd been leaning against. His friend picked up the phone Jax had dropped, and he could hear Sam McCall was filling him in. Kyle waved over Kent and Micah who were just walking in the club's back entrance after their workout. Kyle called to them, "Where are Gracie and Tobi?" The panic in his voice clear and both men took off running for the pool area.

As soon as Jax had his phone back in hand he fired off a text to his younger sister. Elza was a loving young woman, and far too trusting if you asked her older brother. Her profound deafness made her particularly vulnerable to the dangers of living in a large city, but she'd stood rock-solid against what she called her family's attempts to keep her wrapped in cotton. Jax realized Kyle was already making calls, but Jax wasn't able to focus on anything but his phone's infuriatingly blank screen. When she finally responded that she was at their parent's home, Jax had been grateful he was already sitting because the relief that flooded him would have folded his knees out from under him. *"At mom and dad's. Flu. Needed TLC…Why? What's up?"* *Never thought I'd be happy my baby sister had the flu, but damned if I'm not downright thrilled.* He'd tapped out a quick get well soon message and then called his dad filling him in on the threat to Elza's life. His parents' home was a virtual fortress and Jax didn't doubt it would be impregnable within the hour.

According to Sam, the only things the intruder hadn't destroyed in Jen's small apartment were the few items she'd secured in the wall safe and what she kept packed in her panic bag stored in the hidden space between the floor joists under her bed. Sam's voice had been filled with admiration when he'd described how well concealed the compartment was. And Jax was damned proud of her as well. He was also thrilled that she'd followed his suggestion. The only time he'd visited her apartment in D.C. had been right after she'd moved in, and he'd told her the wooden floor in her bedroom would work perfectly for a place to hide a bag of essentials. Jax had given her suggestions for various items to place in the "escape or panic bag" and he was beyond proud of her for following through.

Jax's dad had called him three times wanting Jennifer brought to the McDonald estate at the edge of Austin. Jax understood why his dad wanted her under his roof because Bill and Carol McDonald considered her one of their own, but Jax also knew they'd have a much better chance of resolving the situation if she was at Prairie Winds. Not to mention the fact Jax knew his friends well enough to be certain they weren't going to let the little trouble magnet out of their sight. Jax had never seen Sam or Sage McCall show the slightest hint of interest in a woman beyond an evening of mutually shared pleasure. But he'd seen a change in both men after they'd accompanied Jen home from Costa Rica. The flicker of possession in their eyes had been unmistakable.

Bill McDonald hadn't become successful in the oil fields by being a pushover and Jax had finally been forced to recruit his mom to convince his dad that six former Navy SEALs were perfectly capable of looking out for one woman, even if that woman was Jennifer Keating. Jax smiled as he thought about how quickly Jen had become a part of their family. In his opinion, the love and commitment they'd consistently shown Jen spoke volumes about the kind of people his parents were. He'd already been in the SEALs when she'd come into Elza's life, but he and Micah had fallen under her spell that first Christmas and she'd been a second sister from then on.

Jax knew his parents had funded Jen's education. They'd made her sign loan papers each year and taught her how to budget her money. They'd crammed a lifetime's worth of lessons in just a few years. During her graduation party after finishing her master's degree, he'd watched as they set fire to all the loan "notes" in the backyard fire pit. He'd laughed at her shocked expression. How she'd ever thought they'd let her repay them was a mystery to him. In short, the sweet little woman with the smart mouth and brilliant mind had become a part of their family in such a fundamental way he couldn't imagine how they'd gotten along without her.

He and Micah had worked non-stop for the past several hours. Between their regular duties at the club—which had been busier than any normal night, and handling details for the D.C. trio's return to Texas via private transport, Jax felt like he'd been run over by a truck—a very large truck that had backed up and hit him a second time just for good measure. Waiting for the private elevator that would take them upstairs to the Wests' private condo where Gracie was resting under Tobi's watchful eye, Jax looked in the mirrored doors and groaned. "Jesus, I look like shit. Hope I don't scare our wife."

Next to him, Micah chuckled, "I'm not sure that's possible after the evening she's had." When Jax looked over at his best friend with a brow raised in question, Micah explained, "Tobi sent me a text about an hour ago. Gracie's been sick off and on all evening. I called Doc Brian and he suggested an electrolyte drink, which Regi went to get for her. I haven't heard how it's working, but he wants to see her in their office first thing in the morning regardless."

Jax was grateful Kirk Evans and Brian Bennett had recently relocated their women's health clinic to a small community just west of Austin. The two physicians were also members of Prairie Winds and well-respected Doms. They were also both prominent ob-gyns and their first-hand understanding of the dynamics of D/s relationships made them perfect choices for Gracie's care. And knowing Gracie's prenatal care was being handled by doctors who wouldn't report them to the local authorities if he or Jax threatened to paddle her ass for not taking care of herself was more important than anyone outside the lifestyle might imagine.

Stepping into the Wests' opulent living room, they looked up to see Tobi headed their way shaking her head. "Shhhh. She just fell asleep. Are you sure you don't want to just leave her here tonight? I hate to disturb her. She really does need to rest." Jax was torn but in the end he wanted her between them and he honestly believed Gracie would rest better in her own bed. Besides, she was theirs to shelter and nurture, and they'd already left her in Tobi's care far too long today.

RAPHAEL BALDAMINO WATCHED from the shadows across the street from Jennifer's apartment building as she left with the two men who had stolen her from him in Costa Rica a year ago. If the idiots who had worked for him had gotten the right woman the first time, she'd have been his this past year. He'd seen her just before leaving for a short trip to the U.S. and had mistakenly assumed the pictures he'd snapped would ensure his men would be able to pick her up without incident. Watching her walk down the street that first afternoon had taken him back to the first time he'd seen Rose. There was a carefree innocence surrounding her, but the light of intelligence had also shown in her eyes.

Jennifer was the perfect contrast to his Rose. Where Rose's long dark hair accented her lightly tanned lush curves, Jen's blonde hair and ivory skin emphasized her petite, slender build. He looked forward to having them both on his arm as he showed them off to the world that had turned its back on him. He saw the repulsion and horror in people's eyes when they looked at him. But it was the pity in the expressions of so many that made him want to reach through their chests and yank out their hearts with his bare hands. How dare they pity him? Respect was what he craved, but that fucking helicopter crash had stolen the gilded life he'd known. The months he'd spent healing had allowed him plenty of time to plan, putting everything into place. And now, after overhearing detectives exiting the building mention Jennifer was returning to a private club in west Texas, Raphael knew it was time. It was time to make his way back to The Prairie Winds Club and reclaim the two women who belonged to him.

Chapter Twelve

J EN WAS NUMB. She'd gone through all the motions—
answered all the questions and somehow managed to
remain focused until she'd looked down at the duffle that
served as her "go bag" and realized that aside from her car,
everything she owned was now contained in the small
black satchel. Staring at it, she felt the tidal wave of emotion she'd been holding back finally break free and this time
she didn't make any attempt to push out of Sam's embrace
when his strong arms encircled her.

"It's okay, pet. Let it out. We've got you." Sam's words
were all it took for the dam that had been holding her tears
to crumble and she just cried until she felt completely
drained. She let him comfort her and once she settled he'd
wrapped her in a blanket scented with the sweet jasmine
Jen associated with Betty's large corner apartment. Jen
hadn't even tried to argue when Sam had picked her up
into his arms and made his way down to the car idling at
the curb. The last thing she remembered before drifting off
was Sage settling next to them and lifting her feet into his
lap.

Feeling Sam's lips pressing against her forehead as he
murmured soothing words to her lulled her into a deep
sleep that set her free from the images replaying in her
mind. The destruction that had greeted her when she'd
stepped into the apartment that had been her sanctuary

faded away, replaced by blissful calm. Jen had been independent since her foster mother had died just before her eighteenth birthday. Sure she'd had more than her share of help from the McDonalds, but she'd never felt comfortable putting herself fully in another person's care until this moment. The peace she felt letting them handle things today probably should have mortified her, but it didn't, she hadn't felt anything but sweet relief.

SAM HELD JEN in his arms as they drove out onto the tarmac toward the private jet waiting for them. Rather than stay in D.C. until the McDonald's family jet could make the flight from Texas, Micah and Jax had called in favors and secured alternate transportation in less than an hour. They'd already arranged for Jen's car to be stored and Sam hoped like hell she'd just sell the damned little cracker box and let them replace it with something safer. Folding himself into the little death trap and then letting her hurtle them down the freeway had been a harrowing experience he wasn't anxious to repeat. And thinking about her driving the bright yellow Mini down the open highways of Texas where most of the other vehicles on the road could run over her like a speed bump made him break out in a cold sweat.

Watching the sparkle in her beautiful blue eyes dim over the past few hours had broken his heart. She'd been amazing and held up under the barrage of questions thrown at her from investigators as well as her curious neighbors. When the intrusive inquiries from people in her building seemed to stop suddenly, Sam had ventured out into the hall and found Betty Remly standing guard and turning people away. He'd sent Jax a quick message and Betty would be getting several very nice surprises over the next few weeks from the McDonalds and everyone at Prairie Winds. God, he loved the little geriatric steamroller.

Micah was still trying to get access to the security footage from the days following Jen's departure for Bolivia, and Kyle was using their military contacts to worm their way into the State Department to see if the trip had been a set up from the beginning. If that was the case they had two problems, but Sam had the feeling the man who'd destroyed her apartment hadn't known where she'd gone and that had fueled his anger. But that wasn't to say he hadn't found out and then quickly arranged the embassy takeover. Rubbing his hand over his face in frustration, the truth was that right now he was too exhausted to sort it out.

"You look like I feel." He could hear his brother's attempt at humor, but knew the words were likely true as well.

"Fuck you. I'm beat and worried. And I don't do either one of those gracefully, but you already know that." Sam was usually like a bear with a sore paw if something was eating at him or if he managed to get past a point where he could rest. As a trained soldier, he knew how to push past fatigue, but once he's gone beyond a certain point, he *couldn't* rest, and that usually just plain pissed him off.

The car stopped close to the private jet and Jen stirred as the cool night air moved over her sleep warmed face when the door opened. As he maneuvered her to the door he heard her speak softly, "Please set me down. I need to walk a bit or I'm going to be stiff after the flight." They slipped her shoes back on her dainty feet before setting her down. Sam didn't let go until he was sure she was steady. How the hell women walked in stilettos was baffling to him. They'd wanted to find something more comfortable for her to wear, but all of her clothing had been destroyed save the one outfit in her go bag and she'd said she wanted to save that until they were closer to home. The damned spikes on her feet had given him the perfect excuse to carry her in his arms so he hadn't argued.

The Gulfstream was ready to go within minutes and as soon as the captain gave them the all clear, he and Sage moved Jen into the large bathroom. Sam cupped the sides of her heart-shaped face with his large hands and brushed his thumbs over her flushed cheeks. "Do you trust us to know what you need, pet?"

"Y-yes, S-sir." Sam knew she'd stumbled over the words because his direct question had surprised her, not because of hesitance, and that pleased him. Sage was already naked and had started the shower, but Sam couldn't wait any longer to kiss her. Tilting her face to just the right angle, he pressed his lips to hers and the sweet taste of her changed the chaste kiss he'd planned into a full-fledged plundering in less than a heartbeat. The woman simply unraveled his control on so many levels his mind could barely process them all. Her soft moans of pleasure as she gave as good as she got caused his desire to shoot off into space.

Reluctantly, Sam pulled back from sweet lips and smiled at her lust-fogged expression. "Let Sage undress you, pet. And then we're going to enjoy a shower before we take you to bed and fuck you into oblivion. My brother and I both need to feel your body wrapping itself around ours." He brushed his lips softly over hers, and watched her eyes dilate even further. "And I think you need that connection as well. Tonight isn't going to be about elaborate bits of D/s protocol. Tonight is going to be about two

Masters reading your body's signals and providing exactly what is needed."

Turning Jen into his brother's care while he stripped gave Sam a chance to regain some control over the urge pounding deep within him to conquer and plunder. He'd never experienced such a primal response to a woman and there were parts of his mind that were having trouble comprehending all the implications. Deciding to set those concerns aside and enjoy the very naked woman his brother was leading into the jet's surprisingly large shower, Sam stepped in behind Jen and pressed his throbbing cock against her lower back. "Feel what you do to me, pet? I want you with an urgency that humbles me."

"Baby, everything about you makes me want you. You are smart, beautiful, and we could spend the rest of our lives learning about you and never unravel all of your mysteries." Sage's voice was raspy and Sam knew his younger brother was already falling in love with Jen and he could only hope she didn't end up breaking both of their hearts. "Lean your head back, baby, and let Sam wash your hair. You're going to love it. His fingers are going to massage your scalp as mine massage and wash the rest of you."

Jen leaned her head back and Sam's cock hardened even more as he watched the graceful arch of her back that displayed her ass in all its perfection. He hoped he'd managed to hold back the groan he'd felt rumbling up from his soul as he took in the wonder of Jennifer Keating but knew it wasn't likely. Everything about her appealed to him. Sage had been right when he'd mentioned her intelligence first, because the light of brilliance shining bright in her eyes was a major turn on. But there was so much more to her than that. The way people responded to her, as if they were magnetically drawn into her personal space, fascinated him.

Watching her interact with her elderly neighbor had been like looking into a window of her soul. She'd waited as the elderly woman had taken several rather significant narrated mental road trips during their discussion, but Jen had never tried to bring her back to the topic and had never shown the slightest bit of impatience. Those were the kinds of people skills that are rarely learned, they are innate—just a basic part of a person's personality. Anyone who talked to Jen had every bit of her attention and they knew it. That focus was flattering to even the most hardened skeptic.

Feeling the wet, silken strands of her hair slide between his fingers was one of the most erotic experiences of his life and he'd been involved in scenes that would have singed the hair of most of the Bible thumpers he knew. Seeing the shampoo's bubbles cascading through her long locks before dropping like a plunging waterfall onto the top curve of her ass was sending all his blood south in a big hurry. Watching the suds wash over those perfect curves before streaming down her muscled legs was hypnotizing and Sam had to make a concerted effort to refocus his attention on his task. *Hell, if I'm not careful I'm going to use up the entire three hour flight just watching fucking soap bubbles run off her.*

Once they'd finished their shower, he and Sage had patted her skin dry and then led her back into the jet's bedroom. Settling her in the middle of the bed, Sage moved along her right side and Sam took the left. Circling her peaked nipples with their fingers, both he and his brother just watched her for several long seconds. Seeing her pulse speed up at the base of her neck and watching as her chest heaved with sharp intakes of breath, Sam observed, "You are so responsive. Your body craves our touch and that pleases us both very much, pet." Leaning forward, he licked a circle around her nipple and then blew a puff of air over the damp flesh watching as it drew even tighter. "Have you ever used nipple clamps, sweetheart?"

"No. And I'm not sure I'd like them because my nipples are very sensitive." He appreciated the fact that she hadn't just given him a one-word answer his question had actually invited.

"And that, my pet, is exactly why you should try them. We'll save that for another day, but keep in mind there are a lot of different kinds of clamps. And seeing jewels the color of your eyes dangling from delicate gold chains swinging free as my brother fucks you from behind is something I'm looking forward to very much. Hearing your soft sighs become ragged pleas for release as their gentle tugging ramps up your arousal to the point you don't think there is any way you can take another moment of the torment will be music to my ears, love." He saw Sage's smile when she instinctively arched her back as if seeking the stimulation he'd just described.

"I'm a breast man, pet. I promise you that very soon I'll be able to make you orgasm just from my very intimate knowledge of your breasts. I'll take great pride in knowing just where to touch them to bring about the response I'm seeking." Tracing his fingers over the gentle outside curve, Sam watched as goose flesh moved over her skin in a wave. He chuckled, "See, pet? Your body just told me now much you enjoyed that particular caress."

Sage scooted down the bed and positioned himself between her thighs. Pushing her legs far enough apart to accommodate his broad shoulders, Sam watched Sage wrap his hands around her delicate ankles and fold her legs up until her the bottoms of her small feet were flat on the mattress. "Guess what my specialty is, baby." When she groaned and tilted her pelvis up ever so slightly Sam knew the move hadn't been deliberate, but it did tell them she was going to be a wiggly one so he sure hoped she enjoyed bondage. Sage must have had the same thought because he'd moved his hands under her bent knees and was holding her in a firm, but not a punishing grip. "Your pussy is swollen and a lovely dark pink, baby. It's dripping with your sweet syrup and I can smell your arousal."

"Oh God. Please." Sam grinned at his brother and placed his open palm over her lower abdomen so he'd be ready to hold her because he knew she was going to come clear off the bed when she felt Sage's tongue slide between her sex's tender folds.

"Such sweet begging. I really do love the sound of that, don't you?" Sam watched as Jen's eyelids drifted to the perfect half-lidded position.

"Oh, indeed I do. Let's see what other wonderful responses we can illicit." Sam knew the instant Sage put his tongue against her sex because she'd attempted to arch up with surprising strength just as he'd known she would. And her response to being held against the bed was perfect. Sam felt her stomach muscles quiver just beneath her ivory skin and her blue eyes had nearly rolled to the back of her head. Sam returned his mouth to her nipple, orally seducing the sensitive tip until she was panting from their combined ministrations.

Sam moved up so his lips were near the shell of her ear and ran the tip of his tongue along the outer rim and felt her begin to shake as her body rocketed toward release. "You are getting close, aren't you, pet?" He hadn't expected her to answer, hell she was so deep in her arousal he seriously doubted she'd be able to. Since Jen didn't have any experience in holding back her orgasm, he wouldn't require it tonight. After the adrenaline crest her body had dealt with today, pushing her right now would simply be setting her up for failure and that wasn't the way he and Sage preferred to deal with subs. Punishing a submissive for rules they didn't know or couldn't possibly follow was a sure way to destroy any trust a Dom had built.

Their goal tonight was for Jen to once again associate their touches and attention with mind-blowing pleasure, so pushing her slowly toward orgasm and then making sure it was triggered specifically by their actions was their goal. "Just a few more seconds and we'll send you over into a pleasure so deep you'll scream out our names, pet. But first we both want just a few more seconds to enjoy the gifts you've given so beautifully." Rolling her tight nipple between his fingers, Sam saw Sage's barely perceptible nod and knew he was going to send her over. Sam moved to her shoulder and bit down lightly at the sensitive spot where her slender shoulders joined her neck, and growled against her satiny skin, "Come for us, pet."

Jen's scream was a lusty cry that went straight to his cock and Sam worried for the first time since he was fifteen he was going to shoot his load without ever getting inside the woman he was pleasuring. Every gasp and every cry of their names pushed him closer and closer to the edge of his control. Sage rolled on a condom and was positioned over her before she'd even fully recovered, and from the look of ecstasy on his brother's face as he thrust into her heat, Sam knew her vaginal walls were still pulsing around him.

"Oh fuck, baby. You are so tight. Your pussy is still rippling from your release, but I'm going to take you straight up the mountain again." Sam watched as Sage set a slow pace, thrusting in and then pulling back without hurrying despite her pleas.

Sam maneuvered himself so he was brushing the end of his throbbing cock against her cheek. She turned and pushed the tip of her tongue into the slit and scooped out the pre-cum that was glistening there. "Suck me, pet. I want to see my dick sliding in and out of your sweet mouth. When I come, I want you to take every drop." She'd nodded and hummed her assent. The vibrations of her humming and the soft groans of her arousal were going to send him into space quickly. "Brother, you better be close because our woman's mouth is going to be my undoing in record time."

"Fuck! Already there. Oh, shit." Sage thrust twice more and then went completely rigid. Jen's entire body responded and she screamed around his cock as she came again. The sound waves were just enough to kick him into a white-hot release that stole his breath as well as his ability to think. Sam felt as if his head was about to explode as his cock throbbed sending jets of cum splashing against the back of Jen's throat. She swallowed greedily and Sam fell to the side grateful his arms weren't responsible for holding his weight off the woman who had just turned him inside out.

Sam could see the muscles in Sage's arms quivering and knew the monumental effort it was taking for him to hold himself up so he didn't flatten her into the mattress. *Glad it's you and not me, brother, because there isn't a chance in hell I'd be able to do that right now. Hell, I'm lucky I am still able to breath.*

Chapter Thirteen

TOBI STOOD IN front of the windows watching as the last car made its way up the driveway. It was the darkest hour of the night and she sent up a quick prayer that each of the club's staff and members made the drive to their homes safely. She always worried about those who had to drive any distance, and appreciated that her husbands requested any of their staff that they felt were particularly tired stay in one of the guest cabins. The Prairie Winds property had originally been a guest ranch with accommodations for up to a hundred of people in small cabins and bunkhouses. Some of those had been converted to other uses, but many were still available.

The economic downturn had forced the owners to sell, but when Kent and Kyle bought it, the former owners had stayed on as caretakers. Thinking about Don and Patty Reynolds made Tobi smile and glancing over at the wooden chest Don had restored for her, she felt her eyes fill with tears. The chest had been a gift from her grandmother and was filled with the very few family keepsakes she had. The fire in her apartment had singed one side of the box, but Micah Drake had recognized its importance and brought it to Prairie Winds after the fire. The damage to her apartment had been extensive and Tobi was still grateful that Micah had looked beyond the obvious and seen the beauty of the small wooden chest. Micah had also met Gracie that night, and recognized her beauty and the potential there as well. Gracie had been mad as a wet hen and had gotten right up in Micah's business when she found out he'd been asking questions about her friend among their neighbors.

Having her best friend as part of the Prairie Winds family was a huge blessing. Since Gracie, Jax, and Micah lived next door and they all worked together, the bonds between them had only strengthened. Watching her feisty friend be completely leveled by nausea was heartbreaking. Wrapping her arms around herself, Tobi shuddered and muttered softly to herself, "I swear she's gonna throw that baby up if somebody doesn't do something soon." Strong arms came around her and pulled her back against a rock hard chest. *Kent.* Even though her husbands were identical twins, Tobi could tell them apart by their touch alone.

"What was that, sweetness?" His question was more of a distraction than a real inquiry because Tobi knew full well he'd heard her. *I swear he and Kyle both have dog-ears.* But his lips pressing against the column of her neck in a string of kisses from just under her ear to the tender spot where her neck and shoulder merged sent a spark of electric need straight to her girly parts and the only response she could manage was a moan of pure need. "Well, now I do love that sound. Did you hear that, brother? I think our wife has been lonely this evening." *Yes, lonely...very lonely...and horny...don't forget horny.* It hadn't mattered that she'd tended to her sick friend, she'd still missed her husbands' touch.

Over the past few months, Kent and Kyle had made a dedicated effort to make sure one of them was with her for at least part of each evening, even when the club was open. Tonight had been a rare exception because of all the special arrangements they'd all been making to get Jen and the McCall brothers back home as quickly as possible. Tobi was looking forward to getting to spend more time with Jen, and since she'd be living on-site in one of the cabins, it would be a lot easier. With Gracie out of commission until she felt better, Tobi had been at odds for girl talk. Her mother-in-law, who was also one of her closest confidantes, was on an extended business trip with her husbands and Tobi had been surprised at how much she'd missed having Lilly close every day. Her own mother had died when she was young, but it hadn't taken Tobi long to jump into the deep end of the "I love having a mom" pool. A stinging swat brought her back to the moment.

"I swear, sweetness, you are something else. Where on earth did you go?"

"Wow, it was kind of a crazy mental road trip that started out with Gracie then went to Jen and finally how much I miss your mom." She giggled and turned in his arms so she could press her cheek against his chest. Tobi loved hearing his heart beating deep in his chest, there was something about the sound that grounded her and she let that peaceful feeling wash over her. "I missed you tonight. I understood why you couldn't get away, but I still missed you."

She felt Kyle press up against her back, "We missed you too, kitten. I hear you did an amazing job of taking care of Gracie. She is lucky to have you for a friend." Tobi leaned back and turned her face so she could look into his eyes. The love that she saw reflected in their depths brought tears to her eyes. *Damned hormones.* Lifting a finger to capture a tear, Kyle cocked his head to the side, "What's this, love? Are you alright?"

Tobi grinned, "Yes, just emotional." There was so

much more she wanted to say, but she also knew she'd just shed more tears and right now that wasn't what she wanted.

As if he was reading her mind, Kyle looked down and smiled, "I think our wife is in need of a little playtime, brother."

"I agree, but I need a quick shower, first. Sweetness, I'm going to start a fire in the fireplace upstairs. You are to head up there in five minutes. Lose the robe and lay back on the lounger. Make sure your bare pussy is the first thing we'll see when we come through the door. Do you have any questions?"

Kent hadn't really waited for her answer before he turned her into Kyle's embrace and walked away, so he hadn't heard the airy quality of her, "No, Sir, I understand," but Kyle had smoothed his finger over her cheek and smiled.

"You take my breath away, kitten. Each and every time I look at you I am bowled over with the wonder of it all." He pressed his lips against hers and proceeded to make love to her lips with a kiss that stoked the fires of need in her until she felt like her whole body was burning up. "The fire is lit, so you'll be warm enough until we get upstairs. Head on up, kitten, and be ready for us. We've got some catching up to do with you, love." After another scorching kiss he left her panting and needy as he walked away with a cocky grin that told her he knew exactly how he'd left her, the louse. Watching him walk away, her gaze locked on to how yummy his ass looked in the black Wranglers he wore. The soft fabric molded itself perfectly to his cheeks and thighs and she felt another rush of wetness soak her pussy.

Even though they hadn't shared the news of her pregnancy with anyone yet, her body had already begun making some serious changes. She'd ask Kent and Kyle to hold off a bit because she hadn't wanted to intrude on Gracie's moment in the spotlight. And then when Gracie had been so ill, Tobi hadn't wanted to flaunt how wonderful she felt in her sweet friend's face. But the time was rapidly approaching when she wouldn't be able to conceal the secret. *Damn, being short is a pain in my ass.* In the back of her mind, she knew her bump was growing awfully fast for a first time pregnancy and she wondered if the West family's twin genetics wasn't about to make another showing.

Snapping herself out of her reverie, Tobi hurried upstairs. She wondered how long she'd been lost in her thoughts because one of the showers had already been shut off, but she hadn't noticed when that happened. The rooftop patio was one of her favorite places and she appreciated her men choosing it for their time together tonight. She wasn't sure exactly how the two of them always seemed to know exactly what she needed, but she made it a point to thank God each and every day for the gift. Peeling off the short silk robe she'd put on after her shower, Tobi felt like her skin was tingling all over as she settled herself back on the lounger. Imagining Kent and Kyle's touch had her almost panting with need as she placed her bare feet flat on the floor on either side of the lounger's frame. The pose completely exposed her sex to the view of anyone coming through the door. Knowing her bare pussy was the first thing her men would see sent a ripple of excitement through her and just following Kent's simple command was enough to push her toward the submissive state of mind Tobi knew amped up the intensity of her orgasms. *Good God Gertie, I'm already so horny I'm about to jump out of my skin. Oh crapity crap, I read about this. Pregnancy hormones make some women crave sex. Well, if my whole pregnancy is going to be like this, it's a good thing I've got two husbands.* She'd tried to suppress the happy giggle that bubbled up, but knew she hadn't been entirely successful and didn't really care.

KENT HADN'T BEEN terribly surprised to see Tobi still standing in their living room downstairs when he'd gotten out of the shower, but he'd been shocked that he was able to walk past her without her noticing. That sort of inattention to her surroundings was something they really needed to address with her because her safety was always foremost in their minds. She'd actually seemed even more distracted recently and he wondered if that fact could be related to her pregnancy. He made a mental note to check on it before making a federal case of her lack of awareness. The idea that she might be even more vulnerable while expecting terrified him and he knew Kyle would be equally worried.

He'd positioned himself in the shadows and watched as she took in the rooftop patio. His brother had left the design of the entire apartment to him, but Kyle had claimed control of the roof and the results had been incredible. Kent knew that Kyle was pleased it had fast become one of Tobi's favorite places to relax. The fireplace was perfect to take the chill out of the air and they were working on a way to cool a small portion of the area as well. They wanted Tobi to be able to enjoy her sanctuary during the scorching Texas summers as well. There wasn't any doubt they would eventually build a larger home closer to the river, but those plans were far enough in the future they planned to make the modifications to the roof as a surprise for their sweet wife.

Kent felt his brother step up beside him and smiled because Kyle had used the same secret entrance Kent had used earlier. Tobi didn't know about the small passageway and they weren't planning to tell her just yet because it had given them several opportunities to observe her without her knowledge. One of the incredible things about Tobi was that if she was going to act out or misbehave, she would do it right in front of you, there didn't seem to be a deceitful bone in her body. He and Kyle had compared notes and were both amazed they never had to wonder who she was when they weren't looking, because she was one of the most genuine women they'd ever met.

"She loves the garden and I can't tell you how much that pleases me." Kent smiled at Kyle and nodded.

"That she does. Look how wet her pussy is, you can see her cream glistening from here. I do want to check to see if the increase in her distraction is a side-effect of pregnancy because I walked right past her in the living room and she didn't notice me." Kyle's eyes went wide and Kent heard the growl of frustration vibrate through in his brother's chest. "I'm not even going to mention it to her until I do some checking. I might give the good docs a call as well."

Kyle nodded and then said, "Let's go. I'm tired and I want to fuck her before we rest. We left her alone all evening to care for Gracie and she deserves a reward for that. Fortunately for us, our ideas about rewards happen to run the same track."

Kent grinned as they stepped from the shadows, "Indeed they do and that is a fortunate coincidence indeed."

They had already agreed to hold off on taking her ass and pussy at the same time until after they'd visited with Brian Bennett or Kirk Evans. Both men would be working together serving as both Tobi's *and* Gracie's obstetricians and the four of them had discussed all the reasons having friends and Doms taking care of their women was a good idea. However, the bottom line was both men were outstanding, both professionally and personally, and knowing their wives and children were in good hands was what was most important. *Of course there is the added benefit of having a doctor that understands what we mean when we threaten to paddle their asses for not taking good enough care of themselves.*

KYLE STEPPED INTO Tobi's line of sight and smiled when her eyes went wide. He could already tell her mind was racing as she tried to figure out how she'd missed them coming through the door right in front of her. "Kitten, is there a problem? You look confused." He tried to keep the amusement out of his voice and wasn't sure how successful he'd been.

"Umm, no, Sir. Not really a problem, I don't think so anyway. But, well, I was wondering how you got up here without me seeing you. Because, I've been watching and trying really hard to pay attention. Even though I seem to be struggling with that a lot lately." The last sentence had been so quiet he might have missed it if he hadn't been looking right at her. She was chewing on her bottom lip, which she only did when she was deep in thought or worried about something. *Time to get that sharp mind focused on something else.*

"Well, I think your focus challenges are something we need to address, but I'd like to leave that for another day if you don't mind. Right now your Masters have another priority." He paused and watched as her pulse and respiration rates both notched up. "You see, kitten, we were both very grateful that you took such good care of Gracie this evening. Your help was critical in that it made it much easier for us do our jobs this evening."

"It also freed Jax and Micah up to make the arrangements to get Jen and the McCall brothers headed this way as quickly and safely as possible. There is quite a story to tell about all of that, but that is also for another time. Because right now we're planning to reward you, sweetness." While Kent had been talking, Kyle had moved to Tobi's side and knelt down next to her and was running his hand over the soft swell of her abdomen. According to the preliminary blood work she was only about six weeks along, but she already had a small mound that would be difficult to conceal much longer. He was already beginning to wonder if maybe there was more than one blessing hiding inside this sweet mama.

Moving his hands up to cup her breasts, he noticed they were already changing as well and the differences fascinated him. "Your body is already changing in amazing ways, kitten. It is going to be a joy to take this journey with you. And I'm grateful you aren't experiencing the same horrible nausea Gracie has been facing." He was rolling her nipples gently between his fingers because they had already discovered the increased sensitivity a couple of weeks earlier. When she arched her back and moaned he chuckled. "You take my breath away, love. Knowing our child is growing in you is a total turn on. And my brother and I both know your tendency to worry about things, so we'll be reminding you regularly how beautiful you are until we're sure you believe it."

Kent had taken his position between her legs and was using his thumbs to separate her folds. "Her pussy lips are so swollen and their color is the most beautiful deep rose. It's easy to see why the ancients compared a woman's sex to the flower of love." Kyle could see Kent begin licking her even though he kept his eyes on Tobi's. *That's it, brother, send her over quickly so we can play. I can't wait to sink into her warmth.* Kent pulled back just a bit and spoke, "Her pussy has a slightly different taste now, sweeter and her juices are thicker. I know you are close, baby, and I want you to come as soon as you are ready. And don't hold back, we want to hear your shouts as you find your release." With those words Kent set his mouth back into her sweet pussy and Kyle leaned forward to begin tonguing her nipples one after the other. Within seconds Tobi was shouting her release and hearing their names on her lips as she came was almost enough to make Kyle come against his own belly. He hadn't lost control of his release since he'd been a teen, but it seemed to threaten regularly since Tobi had entered their life.

Kent moved up Tobi's torso quickly and slid his cock into her channel just as Kyle moved up by her head so that his cock was bouncing against her cheek. "Take me into your mouth, kitten. Suck me in the same way Kent is fucking you." Forcing her to concentrate on matching her movements to Kent's would hopefully distract her enough to let them all enjoy the ride into heaven. It was obvious to him that she was even more responsive now and from what he'd been reading, some women experienced a sharply increased sex drive during pregnancy. If they were lucky enough that Tobi was one of those women, they just might end up with a dozen kids.

Feeling the warmth of her mouth as she sucked hard enough to hollow her cheeks, Kyle felt his eyes roll back in his head. "Holy fuck, kitten. Your mouth is equal measures of heaven and hell. I'm sure heaven can't be any better than this, and I'm having a hell of a time holding on to my control when it feels this good."

"You better be getting close, brother, because her pussy is torturing me. She is so damned hot and, good God, she is so tight I'm not going to last." Their twin connection kicked in and their movements automatically synchronized until the actions of each individual became part of a larger dance that had been choreographed over the eons.

Kyle was sliding in and out of her mouth, pushing a bit farther with each stroke until he was sliding down her throat before pulling back. He could tell his brother was starting to go over the edge so he gave Tobi's nipples a quick squeeze and said, "Come for us, kitten." His words hadn't even been finished when Kyle felt the vibrations of her scream as the orgasm she'd been hovering over took her into its depths with cresting waves. Kent followed her in the time it had taken him to sink into her body as far as he could go. Kyle pushed deep and felt his seed pulsing down her throat in jets so hot he could feel the change in temperature inside her mouth. *Shit. We may not survive this woman. I'm not sure but she may have just incinerated a good portion of my brain cells.*

Chapter Fourteen

JAX HAD HELD Gracie on his lap cuddled against his chest as Micah drove them home and then he'd carried her into the house and she'd barely stirred in his arms. After lowering her gently to the bed, he and Micah stood shoulder to shoulder just gazing down at the wonder laying so peacefully before them. She looked so pale and the dark bruising under her eyes was evidence of how little rest she was getting. When they'd asked her several days ago to describe what she was feeling she'd told them to think about the worst case of motion sickness they'd ever experienced and then double it. Both he and Micah had groaned because it didn't matter how many times you were at sea, every sailor knew there would be one or two excursions that made you violently ill. And the odd thing was, you often had no way of knowing when it would hit or why one trip was different from another. The one thing you *did* know was that it sucked ass.

Just as her eyes fluttered open, Jax heard Micah's phone vibrate in his pocket. His friend glanced at the screen and smiled. "Hey, Brian. No, she is right here, she just opened her eyes and we haven't had a chance to ask her how she's feeling." As if reacting to Micah's words her eyes flew open and she scrambled from the bed and ran into the bathroom. Even through the closed door they could hear the unmistakable sounds of retching. Jax quickly moved into the bathroom to help Gracie, leaving Micah to talk to the doctor. As Jax held her hair and pressed a cool cloth to her forehead he felt lower than a slug's belly because of the hell she was enduring. Finally spent, she curled into a ball on the floor and begged him not to move her. When Micah entered with ice chips she accepted a few but didn't want to raise her head.

"Baby, Doc Brian is on his way over here. He knew you wouldn't want to be taken in to their clinic or the hospital, and truthfully, we'd like to avoid that as well because of the safety concerns we have after what happened with Jen. So he's bringing supplies with him and he or Kirk will be staying until you are settled or we can arrange for a nurse to be here with you."

Watching her tears roll in a silent testament over her pale temples before dropping soundlessly to the tile floor almost gutted him. Jax knew he and Micah were over their heads and he wondered if by chance Lilly West and her husbands had made it home this evening. Leaving Gracie in Micah's care, Jax moved to the living room and dialed the West family matriarch. Feeling a wave of relief when she answered, he quickly explained the situation and felt relief wash through him when she'd promised to be right over despite the fact it was three o'clock in the morning. It wouldn't matter that they only lived a half mile apart, Jax knew at least one of her husbands would accompany her and if he were betting—he'd put his money on both.

An hour later, Gracie had showered, eaten a little bit of soup, which had miraculously stayed with her, and was sleeping comfortably. Brian had examined her and determined that she was just suffering from an extreme case of morning sickness. Jax thought that diagnosis was an understatement considering she was sick anytime she was awake. But Brian had merely smiled and patted him on the shoulder. Jax had wanted to growl in frustration at his friend's attempt to mollify him. Thinking back over the times he'd heard his mother, sister, Tobi, and others complain about being treated in exactly the same way, Jax now had a much clearer understanding of their frustration.

The small pill Brian had given Gracie had done wonders. When their little mama had balked at taking a drug, Brian had patiently explained that sometimes a prescribed medication was preferable to a mother not being able to keep food or drinks down. The effect had been almost immediate and so dramatic that Gracie had declared Zofran was her new best friend.

After Lilly and her husbands left, Jax leaned back in his chair and looked over at Brian Bennett. "What's happening with you guys and Regi?" He didn't see any reason to beat around the bush. Just as well ask what he wanted to know straight out.

Brian sighed and then chuckled, "Hell if I know. I see the desire in her eyes, but something is holding her back. Truthfully? I have the impression she doesn't feel worthy of being loved and for the life of me I can't figure out why. Short of hiring an investigator to find out everything in her background I'm not sure we'll ever know. And neither Kirk nor I are willing to go that far for several reasons. But the bottom line is, if she doesn't trust us enough to share her feelings we probably don't have any future together anyway." The defeat in Brian's voice was gut wrenching to hear, particularly when both he and Jax knew exactly what the secret was that Regi was holding back. Jax was tempted to share the information even though it would be an enormous betrayal of confidence since they'd only uncovered the information as part of her pre-employment screening. But in the end, Brian was right, if she wasn't willing to trust them, building a one-sided relationship would never work. They didn't work in the vanilla world, and they damned well didn't work in D/s relationships.

Jax was surprised when Micah leaned forward and spoke quietly. "I want you to know I am keenly aware of the implications of what I'm about to share. As the head of security for The Prairie Winds Club I know just about everything there is to know about every member of the club as well as the employees. I consider that information privileged and confidential—always." Micah took a deep breath and then continued, "Even if you investigated, you might not find the information because it is sealed and buried pretty deep. Our military contacts made it possible for us to uncover what we needed to know. Without going into detail, I want you to know that Regi witnessed something that a kid should never have to see. Hell, nobody should ever go through what she did. But it's what she did afterward...her incredible courage and commitment to doing the right thing that I wish she would use as a measure of her value as an adult."

Micah ran his hand through his hair in frustration, "I am only telling you this much because I know as physicians, you and Kirk understand the importance of confidentiality. And I truly think Regi is nearing a crossroads in her life. She has run about as long as she can and the time is quickly approaching where she is going to have to face her past and change the way she views it—and I'd like to see you and Kirk be there to catch her when she falls. Because everything she believes about herself will fall away and she's going to crash and burn. She's going to need someone who believes in her—someone who can open her eyes to what the rest of us already know about her."

Jax was actually stunned. He and Micah had been friends for most of their lives and he'd never known the man to be emotionally driven. Obviously Gracie was having a positive impact on him and it made him wonder what positive changes others were seeing in him. Brian didn't respond for so long Jax was beginning to wonder if he planned to. Standing up, Dr. Brian Bennett simply nodded once in understanding and said, "I know Gracie had an appointment scheduled for later this morning, but I'd rather she got some sleep. I was going to stay, but she is so much better I don't think there is any need to. Just bring her in later in the day and we'll work her in." As they watched him drive away, Jax couldn't help but wonder how he and Kirk would use the information. Only time would tell, but for the first time, Jax felt like Regi might have just been set back on to the right-track.

JEN WOKE UP the instant the jet's wheels touched down on the runway. She wasn't surprised to find herself alone in the large bed, but she *was* surprised at the disappointment she felt. Scrambling to untangle herself from the sheet, she was pleased to see one of the guys had left clothing out for her. Gathering her things together, she darted into the bathroom. By the time the plane stopped moving she'd made herself presentable and reached the bedroom door just as Sam entered. He seemed startled she was up and dressed and it pleased her to surprise him. "Well, good morning, sunshine. You look wonderful. I just checked on you a few minutes ago and you were fast asleep. I'm impressed. My mom swears that all women take hours to get ready. I'm going to enjoy gloating that you have 'outed her'."

"Don't you dare. I don't want to be in trouble with anybody's mother. Since I haven't had one of my own for a very long time, I'm not really very good at that specific dynamic." She watched as he smiled and she felt as if all the air had suddenly been sucked out of the small room. *Oh my God in heaven.* His smile was dazzling and coupled with a body that was the definition of sex on a stick, he was the kind of man that made New York ad agencies millions of dollars.

When she realized she was staring, she tried to move past him, but his hand wrapped around her bicep stilling her. "We're going to talk about that look, pet. You were looking at me like you wanted to eat me alive—and I liked it very much." She knew her surprise had shown when he grinned at her before leaning down and kissing the tip of her nose. "You are a delight. You're face broadcasts everything in the most amazing ways." He gave her another kiss, this one to her forehead before whispering against her ear, "And that calls to a Dom in ways you can't even begin to imagine, pet."

The drive to Prairie Winds passed quickly with Sam and Sage updating her on what little they'd discovered while she'd been sleeping. The security footage from her building was routinely recorded over after a week, so anything of value had been lost to that cost-saving measure. Though disappointing, it hadn't surprised her that much. Sam unfolded a piece of paper and placed in front of her. She studied the sketch of a man with a badly scarred face and looked up at Sam. "Do you recognize this man, pet?"

"No. Where did you get this picture? The sketch is very

good."

"Your sweet neighbor is quite the artist. And despite her advanced age, her training runs bone deep, love. She remembered every nuance of her encounter with this man. She described his mannerism, the inflections in his voice. Tone qualities that indicate he is Hispanic but hails from the Pacific coast of Central America." Jen just blinked at him trying to bring his words into line with the woman she knew…the one who called her from the local grocers to ask her to shut off her shower because she'd run to the market for shampoo and left the water running. It was hard to imagine the Betty she knew as the focused operative Sam was describing. "I can tell by your deer in the head-lights expression you have forgotten that intelligence is rarely generalized. More often than not it's quite specific and if you are dealing out of someone's area of expertise, they can actually be quite average and sometimes they can even appear somewhat dim. But the significance here is that Betty knows her value as an operative so she keeps those skills sharp. Did you know that despite her claims to the contrary she is actually still helping out the agency quite regularly? That is why she doesn't move closer to her son—because she knows the work she does is important."

Jen took several seconds to absorb the information and then just leaned her head back and laughed. Letting the humor of the situation move to the front of all the challenges of the past week helped her put things in perspective. She could hear her foster mother's voice ringing through her mind reminding her to not take herself so seriously, "Don't go thinking you are all that and a bag of chips, Jennifer. Because the Universe has a way of knowing just when you need to be humbled and it is rarely shy about doing it."

Both Sam and Sage were looking at her with amused curiosity and that just seemed to fuel her giggles. When she was finally able to control herself enough to speak, she explained Millie's words of warning and shook her head. "I was so proud of my *important* position at the State Department. I talked to Betty endlessly about all the great things I was working on. And all the time she had all these amazing stories I should have been listening to. She's seen so much and done so many incredible things and she never said a word about still working. She just praised my measly efforts and let me think I was oh so important." Her giggled had faded as shame and embarrassment washed over her. "Fuck me! What a self-absorbed ass I've been."

"Stop. Now. Betty pulled me aside and told me to expect this. She also said to tell you that she is very proud of the woman you've become. You have no idea how amazing she thinks you are. She also insists that you call her after talking to Kyle and Kent West. They are putting together a team of operatives and well, hell, she knew more about the project that I do—so don't talk to me about being humbled." He snorted a laugh and shook his head.

Sage leaned forward and pulled her hand between his own. "We are close to Prairie Winds and we'll get settled in the guest house before meeting with Kent and Kyle tomorrow morning. They are having dinner with his parents tonight and then they'll be working. The club will be open tonight. Would you be interested in walking through and checking it out? We'd be very careful where we take you because you haven't been interviewed by Micah or the Wests yet, but they've given us the okay to make a quick tour. It would give you a chance to see a few scenes." Jen felt her face grow hot and suddenly her panties were soaked. Did she want to see all the things she'd read about? Would reality beat her imagination? Could anything beat her imagination? *Doubtful.* But damn, just thinking about seeing what skin looked like as the leather of a flogger thudded rhythmically against it bringing the blood to the surface and sensitizing each inch as the frequency and intensity of the strikes ramped the sub higher and higher until… "Damn, brother, I wish like hell I knew what was dancing around in that beautiful head of hers. But I'm pretty sure her reaction means she is more than a little bit interested in touring the club." *Uh huh, yep…me over here….color me very interested.*

Chapter Fifteen

S AGE LOOKED DOWN at Jen as they entered the club's front entrance just in time to see the small shiver that worked through her like a subtle but deep wave. Sage had always loved watching those ripples move through a sea that appeared calm on the surface but were moving mountains of water just out of sight. It would have been easier to enter through the back, but both he and Sam wanted her to get a feel for the dynamics of the Prairie Winds Club so they'd taken the extra time to make their way around the large main building. Tank and Regi were at their usual posts in the club's large reception area, both looked up and flashed smiles as the three of them entered. "Welcome back. Masters Kyle and Kent mentioned you might be coming in this evening." Regi skirted the counter that separated them and wrapped her arms around Jen. "Damn, girl. What a week you're having, huh? You need to move back to Texas where all these big bad retired soldiers can watch your back. Besides, we really could use another girl on our team, geez, the ratio has gotten completely out of hand."

Sage shook his head at her silly patter, but appreciated the fact Regi's easygoing humor had made Jen feel welcome and appeared to have taken the edge off her nervousness. When he and Sam had agreed to join the Prairie Winds staff, Kent and Kyle had explained that

Regina Turner had worked for them since they'd opened the club. They'd also said they thought she used humor as a shield. Sage had wondered more than once what kind of trauma she'd experienced and he could only hope that someday she'd let someone close enough to help her find peace. In Sage's opinion, helping submissives work through issues so their lives were improved was one of the best parts of being a Dom. It was often a daunting task for both the sub and the Dom, but over the years he'd seen lives changed for the better because the people involved hadn't given up.

Stopping Jen just before they entered the main room, Sage turned her so he could look into her eyes as he spoke, "Baby, I want you to listen very closely. Remember, that visitor's band on your wrist will only protect you from being punished by another Dom. If you are deliberately rude or disrespectful, another Dom can and probably will request that you are punished in a way he or she feels remedies the problem." He gave her a few seconds to process his warning and when she gave him a quick nod he kissed her forehead. "I don't want to frighten you because there are a lot of really great people in the lifestyle. But you are impetuous and accustomed to speaking your mind, and I don't want to see that come back to bite you in the ass tonight."

"That's right, pet. Tonight is about learning and giving you a chance to see what the club is about. We won't leave you alone and we'll answer all of your questions, but you need to keep them respectful. Also, speak quietly enough that only we hear what you are asking."

She looked both of them in the eyes and nodded. "I understand, Sirs. I have done a little bit of reading about protocol. I'm not an expert and I know there is a big difference between studying something and having practical experience, so I appreciate your reminders. I'm hoping Tobi is here tonight, she promised to show me around a bit too."

Sage smiled at her, "I think she and her Doms will be along in a little while. They were having dinner with the elder Wests but then coming over to the club after that. Now, if you're ready, let's see what you think of The Prairie Winds Club, shall we?"

TOBI WAS THRILLED that her in-laws were finally back home. She'd missed Lilly terribly during the past few days. They'd spoken on the phone several times and emailed each other daily, but it wasn't as good as sitting down face-to-face and just chatting. She loved both of her fathers-in-law as well, but she hadn't formed the same bond with Dean and Dell that she had with Lilly. Tobi's friends had teased her about sounding like a sappy greeting card, but Lilly really was the mother she'd missed having for so long. She'd been lost in her thoughts and hadn't even realized they'd arrived at their destination until she felt the pads of Kyle's fingers brushing over her cheek. "Kitten, why the sad expression?"

She felt a tear run down her cheek and quickly brushed it aside. "I'm sorry, I don't really know. I was just thinking about how much I've missed your mom." *Damnable pregnancy hormones. I'm a blubbering mess and I hate that.*

Kent chuckled behind her, "You aren't a blubbering mess, but I will agree the pregnancy hormones have made you much more emotional. But they also seem to have you speaking your thoughts out loud again, and I have to tell you I'm enjoying the hell out of that." Tobi groaned, she'd hoped she had finally broken her habit of giving voice to whatever she was thinking. Looking up, she saw Dean and Dell standing on the porch watching them with indulgent smiles. "Come on, let's go. I can tell our dads already know what this is about. Hell, we never could surprise them with anything."

When they walked into the kitchen Lilly whirled around, her entire face lighting up, "You're here! Oh my God, I have missed you so much." She'd taken several steps in Tobi's direction when she froze in mid-stride. "You're pregnant!" Tobi was actually surprised the squeal Lilly let out hadn't shattered the stemware setting on the counter. "Oh don't looked so surprised, sweetheart, it's written all over you. And I am so happy I can barely contain myself."

Tobi glanced over at Kent and Kyle who were both holding up their hands as if to say they hadn't blabbed but her skeptical expression must have been easy to read because Lilly waved a hand in their direction, "Oh those boys didn't tell me a thing and they'll pay for that I promise you."

"Lilly, my love, maybe you should give Tobi a chance to speak." Dean's drawl was always more pronounced when he was trying to rein in his vivacious wife and for some reason it struck Tobi as funny.

Even though she tried to hold back her giggle, it was useless. Looking around her at the surprised expression on all four mens' faces hadn't helped at all and now she was laughing so hard tears were streaming down her face. But when she'd looked up at Lilly, she'd seen nothing but understanding and that had changed her laughter into sobs. Lilly stepped forward and pulled her into a crushing hug, "Your body is feeding you a mighty powerful hormone cocktail, isn't it, sweet girl? It's okay. Just ride it out, it fades...eventually."

The rest of their dinner had been uneventful, but it was easy to see Lilly was struggling to keep a lid on her excitement. As soon as she'd served dessert she'd asked, "So, how soon until I can tell my gal-pals that I'm going to be a grandmother? I can hardly wait. Several of them have been waving pictures of their grandchildren in front of me for years. It's time for some serious paybacks." Tobi couldn't help but giggle as she quietly did a mental happy dance that her new family was all home.

Chapter Sixteen

THE FIRST THING Jen noticed when they stepped into the club's main room was the smell of leather and the second was the fact that aside from the clothing, or lack of, the room looked a lot like the many other clubs she'd been to and a whole lot like the pictures she'd received. She hadn't been thrilled about giving up her shoes, but evidently it was some kind of rule that submissives were supposed to be barefoot. Regi had explained that there were certain theme nights where the subs could wear fuck-me shoes, but then she'd rolled her eyes and added, "I don't bother because I am such a klutz I'd end up with broken bones for sure. Or flashing everybody in the place when I fell."

Sam and Sage had stopped just inside the large double doors at the entrance giving her a chance to take in the room before she felt Sage's hand at the small of her back urging her to follow Sam. Jen was amazed at how people seemed to just part and let them walk through. She'd always been small and hated struggling to make her way through crowds. She couldn't help but wonder what it would be like to be able to see over the other people and to have them just move aside so you could pass. She was surprised when Sam ordered her a small margarita after Sage had picked her up and settled her on one of the bar stools. Giving voice to her observation, she said, "I'm surprised they serve alcohol." Just then the bartender returned with her drink and a wristband, which he quickly secured to her wrist.

Sam leaned down and spoke against her ear in order to be heard over the music, "Be mindful of your manners, pet."

She knew she must have looked confused, because she was...until it hit her. "Oh...I'm surprised they serve alcohol, Sir." She didn't really understand why she felt so validated by Sam's quick smile and simple nod, but she decided to worry about it later.

He leaned close and answered, "There are very strict guidelines about drinking. There is a two drink maximum and you are not allowed to play after you've had anything with alcohol. Since you are a visitor and not allowed to play anyway it isn't an issue. And hopefully it will help you relax a bit before we look around." He pressed his lips against the sensitive skin just below her ear and Jen felt goose bumps pebble over her skin.

She'd been so busy taking in everything around her, Jen hadn't realized she'd finished her drink until Sage took the glass from her and set it on the bar. "Come on, baby, let's see what interests you, shall we?" He and Sam had been standing on either side of her as she'd looked around, but the room was crowded enough that she really hadn't been able to see much beyond the small sitting area directly in front of them.

The first scene area they approached had a buxom young woman tied to what Jen recognized as a St. Andrew's Cross. The man who was flipping the leather strands of a flogger over her breasts was totally focused on his task and the woman's eyes looked like she was free-floating in a daze. Watching as the Dom paused to check her bindings before speaking quietly to her, Jen read the woman's lips and knew she'd answered "Green, Sir" to whatever the man had asked her. The Dom was probably six feet tall, but it was the black leather boots, pants, and vest he was wearing rather than his physical size that screamed power. He was a nice looking guy, but she didn't find him appealing beyond that. And that surprised her because he was exactly the physical type she'd always found appealing before. It suddenly struck her that her taste in men had shifted since meeting the McCall brothers and something about that was a bit unsettling to her.

"What was that thought, doll?"

"Umm, nothing really. I was just watching and well, I noticed..." Jen wasn't sure she wanted to share everything she'd been thinking, but quickly decided they would know if she lied. And really, she'd learned that trying to present yourself as something you aren't in order to win a man's approval always cost her more in the end, so if it turned out to be a problem, then it was theirs and not hers.

"Eyes on me, pet." When she looked up at him, he continued, "Finish what you were saying. And remember, partial answers are not acceptable."

"Oh, yes, I'm sorry....Sir. I was just thinking the Dom over there is exactly the physical type I was always attracted to...well, before. And it surprises me a little that my tastes have changed since meeting you and your brother." Sam's eyes softened and his smile was bright enough to have powered every light in the room.

"That pleases us more than you can imagine, love." Anywhere else the scorching kiss he'd given her would have seemed completely inappropriate, but considering where they were it was easy for her to just relax into the moment and enjoy the passion that was practically pulsing around both men. When his lips pressed against hers, their warmth felt as if it was spreading and the burn was from the sexual tension alone. As his tongue slid along hers, Jen felt her knees start to shake and she was grateful he'd wrapped one arm around her back while his other hand was cupping the back of her head. She wasn't sure whether it was the ambiance of the club, the small bit of Dominance he was showing her, or the satisfaction she felt at having pleased him, but Jen felt the thong she was wearing dampen. She hoped it wouldn't be noticeable under the obscenely short skirt they'd given her to wear, but given the way Sam's hand was sliding down her ass, it was doubtful her arousal would be a secret much longer.

"Are you wet for us, pet? If I slide my hand under your skirt will I feel your heat before I even move my fingers under the edge of your dainty panties?" Jen wanted to answer, but when his fingers made their way into her folds, every thought fled from her mind.

Sage pressed close and moved his hand under her skirt, pressing under the front edge of her panties to draw lazy circles around her clit. "Oh, baby, you are so close. Do you want to come? If you do, you need to ask nicely because those orgasms now belong to your Masters." *Masters? My orgasms belong to them? I don't think I want them to have that much…Oh my stars and garters…* It was the last thought she had before Sam's lips pressed against hers catching her cry and the world around her exploded in a release so powerful her knees folded just as white light lit the inside of her eyelids.

SAGE KNEW SAM hadn't wanted to give her the release, but she'd likely be getting several swats for not waiting their permission. Sage knew full well he'd pushed her over the edge just because he's wanted to feel her come apart in their arms, and come apart she had. And even though it made him an ass, he didn't regret it because feeling her buck in their arms as her warm syrup slid over his fingers in the middle of the club's main lounge was just about the hottest fucking thing he's ever experienced. Sage felt Sam's hand moving against his own as he pulled his fingers from her channel, so it seemed Mr. Always in Control hadn't been able to resist Jen either.

"Master Sam, I do believe our sweet sub just came without permission." He wasn't going to tell her that they had technically just violated the club's rules against playing with a visitor.

"You know, I was just thinking the same thing. But since we can't punish her here, I guess we'll have to wait until we get back home to administer the swats she's just earned." Sage had been able to hear the amusement in Sam's voice and wondered if Jen had as well.

Just then he heard Tobi's voice beside him, "Master Kyle, isn't it against the rules for Doms to play with visitors?" Damn, wouldn't it just figure they'd get busted by the club's owners? The little vixen knew full well it was against the rules, but she was going to make sure Jen knew it as well. "I know I still have a lot to learn so I am just checking, Sir."

Sage heard Kyle's snort of laughter before he answered, "Kitten, you are skating on extremely thin ice, best tread very carefully. But in answer to your question, yes, you are correct. And since I'm sure these two Doms wouldn't punish a visiting sub for a rule violation if they were also guilty, I think we should just move along. I see my brother has things set up on the stage for us. I'd like to get this announcement made so we can go upstairs and celebrate."

SAM HAD BEEN completely shocked at his and Sage's lack of control. Making Jen come in the middle of the club's main room had been a completely selfish act as well as a very clear violation of the rules. Hell, their friends would be well within their rights to fire them before they ever started. He knew they wouldn't, but Sam wasn't the sort of man who usually just blew off rules, particularly when they were in place to protect the woman in his care. *Jesus, what a Charlie Foxtrot.* He'd known both he and Sage were on edge before they ever left their cabin, but he was also certain that would be the case every time they walked into the club. The cluster fuck they'd created wasn't going to be easy to fix. If they abruptly changed tactics—which was what they *should* do, then Jen was going to feel as if she'd done something wrong and they were pulling back. But if they didn't, he knew they'd probably have her pinned against the wall and their dicks buried in her within an hour.

Her reaction to the first scene had been so pure in its sexuality, the eroticism of the moment had completely bowled him over. He'd been a sexual Dominant for so long he couldn't remember having sex that didn't involve dominance of some kind. Straight vanilla sex held no appeal for him. Jennifer's reactions to what she'd seen and even the smallest hints of bondage had sent his libido into launch mode and he hadn't even tried to pull it back. Despite the fact they'd been standing in the middle of a room filled with people, Jen hadn't even noticed them. Her attention had been completely focused exactly where it was supposed to be—on her two Masters.

There wasn't any question that Jen was a sexual submissive, but her surrender would have to be earned every single day and that lit a fire in his gut he hadn't even realized could exist. Sam and Sage had known for years they wanted to share a wife. But the most he'd ever hoped for was that Sage would find a woman to love and Sam would feel enough attraction to her that his life would be filled with the joys of family and a sexual relationship that was satisfactory. However, with Jen he knew everything would be different.

They continued walking through the club and the various scenes they watched elicited different responses from Jen. She'd literally hidden her face in Sage's chest anytime they'd been near a scene involving real pain. That wouldn't be an issue, because even though they were considered strict, neither he nor Sage was a sadist. She had been interested in the wax play scene and the ultraviolet light wand, but had turned sheet white when they'd mentioned the piercing room that had recently been setup on the club's second floor. "I'd rather not see that, if you don't mind. I passed out when I had my ears pierced and they didn't even bleed." He and Sage had both burst out laughing and he'd felt bad when he saw how pale she'd turned.

"Doll, we aren't in to those types of play either. I'm relieved to know they don't hold any appeal for you, but I did feel obligated to let you know it's available. From what I've heard Kyle and Kent have serious reservations about it and only recently began offering it. Anyone who wants to schedule the room has to provide proof they have the proper training and certifications in advance." Sage had massaged her shoulders for a few minutes and then given him a quick signal letting Sam know she'd finally relaxed.

Meeting the Wests in the main lounge later in the evening, they congratulated them on their announcement and moved closer to the women's lounge when Tobi requested a restroom break. Sam suspected she was playing the 'pregnant and have to pee all the time card' he's seen his sisters use, but if her Masters weren't calling her on it, then he wasn't going to point it out. Watching Tobi pull Jen along, Sam had to suppress his smile because she'd just confirmed his suspicions.

JEN LAUGHED AS Tobi tugged her into the beautiful lounge as all four men stood guard just outside the door. Tobi turned to her as soon as they were out of earshot, "I just wanted to check on you. That was a super-hot scene we walked up on. Fuck me, I almost came just watching you guys." Jen felt her cheeks heat and knew her damned fair complexion was giving away her embarrassment. "Well pogo-shit, I didn't mean to embarrass you. I forget that not everybody is ready for my blunt way of saying things. Crap, I wasn't this open sexually before meeting Kyle and Kent either. Geez…I'm rattling on and I can see that dazed look in your eyes…actually people get that a lot when I talk to them. Hmmm. You'd think I'd get a clue, huh? But it doesn't seem to be working out that way." Her giggle seemed to break the spell Jen had been locked in and they both dissolved into a fit of laughter and before Jen knew it they were both wiping away tears.

Once they'd finally regained their composure, Jen answered, "Yes, I'm fine although I do feel bad about what happened earlier because I felt like Sam and Sage were just giving me what they knew I needed. I hate that they regret it and I get the sense they feel like they let your husbands down." What she'd failed to mention was that she'd be leaving as soon as it was safe and hopefully before she would jeopardize the life the McCall brothers had chosen. Ruining their reputation as Doms and trustworthy men wasn't a risk she was willing to take. Her lack of control had put them in an untenable position and she wouldn't make that mistake again.

Tobi had stepped back and seemed to be studying her closely. "You aren't taking on the responsibility for that, are you? Because I have to tell you, sister, pregnant or not I will seriously kick your ass if you are owning that. Hell's bells and hand grenades, I know it wasn't supposed to happen, but damn, girl, it was so hot to watch. Mercy! And those guys won't be in trouble for it, they will probably get trash talked forever, but hey, if it wasn't that it would be any one of a zillion other things. If there is one thing I've learned, it is Doms and former soldiers give each other shit like no other men I know. If women talked to each other like that all hell would break loose." They settled on the small sofa and completely forgot about the men waiting for them until the unmistakable sounds of boot steps filtered into their awareness.

Looking up, Jen was shocked to see all four men standing in nearly identical poses. With their feet shoulder width apart and their muscular arms crossed over ripped chests, she fought off the hot flash of lust that threatened to propel her straight into Sam and Sage McCall's arms. *Oh they are way too much for you, girl…time to back off…fast.* Kyle was the one who finally broke the silence, "Kitten, do you realize that you have been in here for a little more than half an hour?"

Jen saw Tobi flinch, "Really? Wow, I'm sorry. We got

143

caught up talking and I didn't pay any attention to the time. I've been missing 'girl time' with Gracie being so sick and Lilly gone, and Jen is so fun to talk to that I lost track of time…Sir."

Kyle's eyes looked like they were searching for patience in the space above Tobi's head and the other three all rolled their eyes at her last minute add on. "You are really pushing it this evening, kitten. Now, we'd like to get you upstairs and I know Jen's men are anxious to get back to the cabin as well."

Kyle held out his hand to Tobi, but she pulled Jen into a quick hug before placing her hand in his. Tobi squeezed her tightly and whispered, "Give them a chance, don't be afraid to reach out and grab ahold of what you want in life. You deserve it even if you don't believe it right now, it's still true." Jen was shocked at how well Tobi had read her. Still reeling from Tobi's words, Jen just sat on the sofa for several seconds in stunned silence until she realized Sam and Sage were still standing directly in front of her. When she looked up at them she could see their desire, but there was something deeper there too…a connection that she'd seen so often in their eyes. But this time there was also something deeper. She'd seen it briefly before, but it was either more blatant now or she was finally willing to acknowledge it for what it was…a promise of what could be…if she was brave enough to embrace it.

Chapter Seventeen

SOMETHING HAD SHIFTED in Jen, and Sam wasn't sure exactly what it was but the change was impossible to miss. There seemed to be a new air of determination surrounding her, as if she'd made an important decision about her future. He could only hope those plans included him and Sage, because they'd known months ago she was the woman they wanted to plan a lifetime around. When she laid her small hand in his the familiar zing of electricity raced up his arm. He felt the same charge each time their hands connected and he knew from the way her eyes went wide, she'd felt it as well. *Good to know I'm not the only one who feels it.* "Come on, pet. We want to get you home and naked."

Sage stepped up beside them and pushed the curtain of blonde silk hair over her shoulder letting his fingers trail through the tresses. "And then we're going to fuck you into oblivion, baby. We'll both be in your body at the same time, taking our own pleasure as we give you yours. There won't be an inch of you that we aren't going to know, to touch, and to own." Sam saw her eyes dilate and heard the small gasp leave her lips before they led her quickly out of the club. Sam was grateful they'd used one of the Wests' side-by-side ATVs because it had made their return trip to the cabin much faster. If they'd had to walk, he was certain they wouldn't have made it through the gardens without taking her at least once, and that wasn't what they had planned for this evening. They would all three be meeting with the entire Prairie Winds team tomorrow morning and Sam knew that meeting had the potential to change everything so he intended to stay in this moment, because tonight she was theirs—to cherish and command. And he could only hope the bond they'd build tonight would be enough to weather the challenges he was certain were headed their way.

As they neared the small cart, Sage turned to her, "Raise your skirt for me, baby." Sam saw her eyes widen, but she did as she'd been told. The outside lights sparkled off her dewy skin and Sam heard her gasp when Sage reached forward and snapped the elastic on both sides of her thong before sliding it from between her thighs, pressing his fingers against the silk as it slid over her sex. "You'll be sitting on my lap, baby, and I don't want anything between your slick pussy and my fingers. Now let's go before I do something foolish like bend you over the seat and slam into you rather than settling you on my lap for what I hope is a very quick ride down the hill." Sam fully intended to make sure their ride was quick indeed.

Driving fast enough that his full attention was required was the only thing that kept Sam from driving right off the path leading to their cabin. When Sage had settled Jen straddled over his lap facing him so he could use his fingers to begin stretching her ass, Sam had been forced to completely tune them out or they'd have never made it down the small incline. He pulled around to park near the back door and noticed how the night's full moon reflected off the river's calm water. The moonlight's soft hue was almost luminescent and if it had been warmer he would have considered beginning their activities outside. He listened as Jen's breathing became more and more frantic and her soft pleas begging Sage to let her come had his cock rock hard—and they hadn't even gotten her inside the cabin yet.

"Do you like that, baby? Do you like having my fingers stretching out that pretty rear hole?" Sage's voice was raspy and Sam knew his brother was skating along a fine edge too. "By the time we get you inside, you're going to be primed for us. Let's go." Sam heard her groan of frustration when Sage pulled his fingers out of her and lifted her to her feet.

Sam stepped up next to her, untied both knots of the halter they'd given her to wear, and then leaned down to draw one of her tightly puckered nipples into his mouth. She arched her back pushing more of her flesh against his mouth and he smiled, "You have the most amazing breasts, pet. They are the perfect size and so responsive." He rolled the other nipple between his fingers while Sage stripped her from the micro-mini leather skirt that had barely covered her ass cheeks. He loved seeing the brief glimpses of the very bottom curve of the globes of her ass as they'd made their way around the cabin. He'd always believed the teasing hints of what was beneath the clothing was far more erotic than full nudity in the club settings. But right now, seeing Jen's ivory skin bathed in moonlight was the sexiest thing he'd ever seen.

Stepping back from her so he could take in everything about her, he was just overwhelmed at the sight in front of him. The woman was simply too beautiful for words and for several seconds all he could do was look at her. "You take my breath away, love. The moonlight washes over you creating light and shadows that showcase every curve. You are simply stunning." Sage stepped up beside her and

Sam saw him go on point just before his eyes darted to the trees off to his left. Sam didn't ask any questions, he just scooped her up and ran up the steps and in the back door as Sage took off toward the trees.

Sam didn't stop until he'd gotten to the smaller of the two bathrooms in the cabin. Since the small space didn't have any windows, it was the safest place for her until they'd secured the perimeter. He quickly wrapped her in a towel and then instructed her to lock the door behind him. "Don't open the door until either Sage or I return for you. We won't be long."

"What happened? Did you see someone?" Sam hated the concern he heard in her voice but he was grateful that she was taking the situation seriously.

"I don't know what Sage saw that set off his alarms, but I trust his instincts. We won't be long, I promise you." He kissed her quickly and then waited outside the door until he heard her press the small lock. As safe rooms went, it was a damned poor excuse, but right now it was all they had.

Making his way toward the back door, Sam heard his brother talking on the back deck and knew he was giving whoever was on the other end of the call the all-clear. "We'll need to check the area tomorrow in the daylight, but it's clear right now. I don't know whether it was a scope or a camera, but whoever it was is a fast mother I'll say that for him." Sage was a hell of a sprinter, so whoever had out run him must have had a healthy head start. Sage finished his conversation and then turned to Sam. "Since you heard my end of it, let's get back to Jen. We'll cover it all in the meeting tomorrow, but for now the rest of the team is patrolling and our focus needs to be on the woman I'm sure we have managed to terrify. Goddamn it to hell, I wanted to get my hands on whoever that was."

When Jen emerged from the small bathroom, Sam was surprised that she didn't seem overly frightened by what had happened despite their sketchy explanation. She'd basically shrugged it off and when he finally asked her about her lack of interest, she'd looked up at him in surprise. "I don't mean to seem disinterested. But you see, this sort of nonsense happens to me all the time so I guess I've become a bit desensitized to it. That is what I was telling you when we were in Bolivia. I just seem to be a magnet for chaos and I've kind of learned to not let things bother me too much...because frankly, it would be exhausting to get caught up in it."

Sam didn't know whether to laugh at the absurd truth of it or growl in frustration at the sheer volume of danger that must have surrounded her to make her seem so blissfully unconcerned about recent events. Deciding kissing her was better than anything he might say, he pulled her against him and slammed his lips to hers. His tongue sought out her heat and didn't leave a single inch of her mouth untouched. She met his passion with her own and stole a bit of his soul in the process. When the need for oxygen finally had him pulling back, Sam looked into her hooded eyes and just took in the wonder of it all. "You undo me. I've never met anyone like you. And your cavalier attitude about your safety is something we'll be addressing very soon, but right now, all I care about is getting the three of us back to the point we were before things derailed."

Sage stepped up behind Jen and slowly unwrapped the bath sheet revealing the very bare and very beautiful woman beneath it. "Oh, baby, you are so beautiful. Everything about you is banging, but the light that shines from the inside is what steals the show." Sam might not share Sage's love of slang, but he certainly agreed with the sentiment. Watching her eyes dilate and the pulse at the base of her neck pick up its pace made Sam hard enough to pound nails. He wrapped his hand around her dainty wrist and pulled her into the bedroom. He only released her long enough to shed his clothes and both he and Sage set new records for getting naked.

Running his hands up and then back down Jen's arms, Sam grasped her wrists and pulled her to the bed. Sage had already arranged the pillows before they'd gone to the club and Sam was grateful for his brother's planning, because each second he was delayed was a second wasted in his view. Seeing her spread out on the bed, legs splayed wide with her pussy lips swollen with desire and glistening with her arousal was enough to take his breath away. Sam didn't have any words in his vocabulary that could adequately describe the connection he felt when looking at Jen. The woman was a dichotomy of submission and strength, and Sam was humbled by the fact she'd entrusted herself to the two of them.

Sam leaned forward, circled the clit with the tip of his tongue, and smiled at her gasp. "Hold still, pet, or I'll stop." Her groan made him chuckle. Sage had laid down next to her and sucked a nipple deep into his mouth. Sam heard Sage's growl of satisfaction and he tasted the sweet cream Jen's body gifted him with in response to their attention. "Well, seems our sweet sub likes that very much." Moving his fingers through her juices, he slid the moisture down until it eased his way into her rear hole. "Let's see how much she enjoys having her ass stretched while we play a bit, what do you say, brother?"

Sage let go of her breast and Sam smiled at the pop that

sounded by the sudden loss of suction. "Sounds like a great plan. I have to get these beauties ready for the jewelry we bought for our lovely sub." Sam pressed his face tight against her sex when he felt her tense at Sage's words. The nipple clamps they'd bought for her would be a gentle introduction into mild pain as pleasure and the small sapphire weights would swing as they fucked her adding to the stimulation. They'd save the connecting chain for another time but he was anxious to see the way the blue stones looked against her skin. They'd chosen the delicate blue stones because they were the same shade as her eyes when she was aroused.

"Judging from the sweet cream she just gifted me with, I'd say she is more than ready." When Sage slid the gold rings over her right nipple and began tightening the little screws that reduced the diameter of the inner ring, Sam redoubled his efforts rolling his tongue and pushing it into her vagina mimicking the motion his cock was going to be making soon. At the same time, he continued stretching her ass so the pain she'd feel when he and Sage were both seated in her body would only be the kind that was a prelude to pleasure.

By the time Sage had tightened the second nipple clamp Jen was panting and barely holding back the release her body craved. Sam was thrilled she was waiting for permission before letting the pleasure overtake her. Though neither he nor Sage had specifically told her to hold off tonight, her body was already attuned to the previous instructions they'd given her. Since they wanted her body and mind both relaxed before they pushed her body with double penetration, he looked up at Sage and nodded. Sage brushed the hair from her face and leaned close enough that she would be able to feel the warmth of his words brush over her cheek as he said, "Come for us, baby." At the same time Sam pushed the fingers of his free hand into her pussy, curving them up so he found the soft spongy spot and caught her clit between his teeth, sending her into orbit.

Chapter Eighteen

G IVING JEN THE command to come for them had been sweet torture. Watching as her entire body flushed and her back bowed off the bed made Sage ache to push into her ass and feel those untried muscles milking his cock dry. Before she had even completely come back to earth he and Sam had taken their positions, rolled on condoms, and positioned Jen so she was straddling Sam's cock. When he'd slid in all the way, Sam groaned. "Fuck. Oh, pet, the walls of your sweet pussy are still pulsing and it feels like you are trying to pull me in deeper. I can't begin to tell you how incredible that feels. You are so very tight and I know I'm going to be fighting a battle with each stroke to keep from coming too soon, because I don't want this to end quickly."

Sage placed his hand between her shoulder blades and gently pushed until she was laying against Sam's chest. Her hiss as her clamped nipples pressed into his brother's chest made Sage smile. That extra bit of sensation was going to serve her well here in a couple of minutes. Sam was leaning at about a forty-five degree angle and that was going to allow them each to have access to Jen's luscious body as they worked together to show her the true magic of a ménage. "Lay against Master Sam, baby. I'm going to make sure your sweet ass is ready to take my cock."

Rimming her sweet rear hole with fingers coated with

lube, Sage was pleased when she moaned and arched her back trying to press closer. When he positioned his cock and started pressing through the tight ring of muscles, he felt her tighten against the intrusion. "No, baby, let me in. Relax and push out. It will only hurt for a few seconds and then the pleasure is going to make that twinge of pain disappear from your mind, I promise you." She did exactly as he asked and their work preparing her paid off as the head of Sage's cock popped through the tight ring.

"Oh ouch...ouch...ouch...ohhh my God." The change in her voice was easy to hear as the pain she'd felt morphed from a singeing heat into one that was pure erotic pleasure.

"Tell us how it feels, pet." Sam's voice sounded strained as he spoke to her and Sage was grateful Sam was distracting her because right at this moment Sage was fighting the urge to plunge forward and couldn't have spoken if his life had depended on it.

"It feels so decadent, naughty, and oh so amazing all at the same time. Master Sage's cock is huge inside me and I'm not sure I'll be able move with both inside me, but I want to...more than I can tell you."

"You're doing perfect, love. Just relax and let us do the work. You only need to *feel*. That is all we require of you, pet." Sam's words had an immediate effect. Sage felt her surrender and it sent a surge of lightning hot desire all the way up his spine. He took his time pushing balls deep and felt sweat beading on his forehead as he struggled to maintain his control.

Once he was in, Sage put his hands over the shoulders and pulled her back against his chest, savoring just how perfectly she fit in his arms. Her soft skin rippled under his fingers and he was thrilled with the way she responded to his touch. "Just let me hold you for a little bit, baby. You are amazing and I just want to enjoy it for a few seconds before we light up your world like the Fourth of July." She shuddered and pressed back against him. He feathered kisses up the side of her neck and then bit lightly on her earlobe. Looking over her shoulder, Sage watched Sam flick the small sapphire weights suspended from the nipple clamps. They groaned simultaneously when Jen's body responded to the sensation by clamping down on their cocks with surprising strength. "Jesus, baby, that felt incredible, but you are pushing the limits of my control to the very edge."

Pushing her back forward just a bit, he positioned her hands so she was braced perfectly between them. The weights could swing free ramping up her arousal as he and his brother took their pleasure from her body. And then, at just the right moment, Sam would slide his hand between them to pinch her pearly little clit and send her over so they would all come at the same time. Sage couldn't wait to feel the intensity of the release they were about to give her. She was so responsive, and the fact they were the first to give her this experience was icing on a very sweet cake. The connection Sage felt with Jen had been intense from the very beginning, but it had become so strong that at times he felt he was almost able to *feel* her emotions. He'd heard Kent and Kyle describe that same bond, but he'd always attributed it to the fact they were twins, so getting even a small glimpse into a connection that strong was eye-opening indeed.

Setting a slow pace, he and Sam worked together. As Sage slid from her tight rear hole Sam would surge deep and then they would reverse. Listening to the soft, sexy sounds Jen made as they worked to overwhelm her was pushing him to the very outer-limits of his control. Watching the muscles in her back and arms work to stay in synch with them was a pleasant distraction, but nothing short of a nuclear holocaust was going to keep him from coming soon. "Baby, your body belongs to us. Your pleasure…your pain. Your future…everything. You. Belong. To. Us." Sage had emphasized the last words with faster thrusts into her tight ass as he lost the tenuous hold he'd had on his control.

"Come for us, love. Come now." Sam's words had the desired effect and Jen clamped so tight on Sage's cock that the first few seconds were an odd mix of pleasure and pain. Letting his release wash over him in crashing waves and watching the explosion of light behind his eyelids, Sage was literally gasping for breath by the time the last hot jets of semen had left his body in what had unquestionably been the most intense sexual experience of his life. In the back of his mind, he'd heard Sam shouting Jen's name and he remembered hearing her scream but the truth was his brain was still not fully functioning, so fitting together the bits and pieces of shattered memory was going to take a few more minutes.

Leaning on shaking arms, Sage kissed and then grazed his teeth over the spot where her neck joined her shoulder. He gave Sam a quick nod and watched as his brother's shaking fingers slowly unscrewed the tightening mechanism on the nipple clamps. There would be times they would use clamps that could be released quickly so the heat of returning blood into the sensitive tips of her breasts would heighten and extend her orgasm. But tonight the plan was to back the tension off slowly so she would associate taking them together with nothing but pleasure. Her soft moans told Sage that even though Sam was being extremely careful, she was still experiencing some discomfort. Whispering against her sweat dampened flesh, Sage hoped to distract her just enough to keep her focus off the throbbing pain she was trying to push back, "Don't fight the heat, baby. Ride it like a wave until you feel it shift into pleasure. Sam is releasing the tension slowly so the discomfort is minimized."

He felt her body stiffen a split second before she groaned, "Do they make testicle clamps? Because I'm thinking that experience might give you a greater level of understanding and compassion." Sage and Sam both chuckled because the words might have been snarky, but the tone had given away the fact Jen was still trying to surface from her post-orgasmic hormone hangover.

Sam unscrewed the second clamp much faster than the first one causing her to arch her back and cry out. "You see, pet? I really was being very gentle. But your smart comments will always be met head on—I promise you." As soon as he'd spoken the words, Sage watched his brother capture her aching nipple in his mouth and lave it with soothing attention. Her gasp of pain soon changed to a groan of pleasure and relief, and Sage grinned at his brother over the gentle slope of her shoulder. She was a joy. Hell, passionate and responsive alone would have been enough to have made her amazing, but with her quick mind and kind spirit added in—she was absolutely perfect.

Sage couldn't wait to introduce her to their family. His sisters were going to love her because, even though she was incredibly beautiful, she didn't seem to be aware of the fact. Her genuine interest in other people would charm even the harshest critic. As he slowly withdrew from her body he settled her on Sam's chest and made his way into the bathroom to clean up and then returned with a warm washcloth to clean her. Sam was whispering soothing words to her when she tried to protest his care, but Sage chuckled when heard her sleepy, "Okay, if it makes you happy knock yourself out," before her entire body went lax and he knew she'd fallen asleep.

Settling down and pulling her into his arms as Sam went to clean up, Sage rubbed his hand up and down the length of her spine pleased with how quickly she pressed tighter against him. "Sage, I feel so safe in your arms. You and Sam spoil me. I wish I could stay right here."

Her words gave him hope that tomorrow's meeting with the rest of the Prairie Winds team might go all right after all. He pressed a kiss to her forehead and whispered, "Me too, baby. Me too."

Chapter Nineteen

JEN STARED AT Kyle West for long seconds without blinking because she wasn't sure whether or not she'd heard him right. The offer he'd just made sounded so perfect that she was certain her imagination was playing tricks on her. *Don't say anything yet. Make sure you aren't hearing what you want to hear and not what he actually said.* Too many times in her life, Jen had listened to someone speak and heard an entirely different message than the one the speaker had actually tried to deliver. One of her foster mothers had called it "selective listening to the nth degree" and Jen had spent several years trying to figure out exactly what the hell that had meant.

She was sitting directly in front of Kyle's desk and Sam was sitting in the matching leather wingback chair to her left. Sage was leaning against the wall off to Kyle's right side, she could almost feel his stare as his eyes remained fixed on her. Jax and Micah were also positioned where they could see her face. The only one who seemed comfortable and his body language was almost screaming his confidence was Kent West. He was reclining on the small sofa with his legs propped up on the coffee table in front of him. When he saw her gaze move over him he chuckled. "I don't know—seems like having an expert in reading body language on board might be a mixed blessing. And knowing she'll be sharing that knowledge with our subs is a bit disconcerting as well." There was something about Kent that Jen had immediately liked. There wasn't a doubt in the world that he was a Dom, but his easy-going rapport with everyone around him made him seem more approachable than his twin.

Kyle West might be a mirror image of his brother, but it was crystal clear he was the more Alpha of the two. Kyle was intense, and often intimidating. Jen would classify his body language as focused and barely leashed while Kent's was much more laissez-faire and relaxed. She'd met both men on a couple of different occasions when they had still been SEALs, but she hadn't had much opportunity to talk with them until after they'd left the teams. One evening when Jax and Micah had been home on leave, she and Elza had decided to spend the weekend at her parents' home so Elza could spend more time with her brother. Jen had gone downstairs late one night to get something to drink and heard men's voices out on the back terrace. When she'd gone to investigate, the four of them were drinking beer and discussing their future business plans.

Kent had looked up and seen her at the door and he'd immediately stood inviting her to join them. She had settled between Micah and Jax listening for several minutes before the conversation turned to specifics about the club the West's were setting up. Jen had felt the heat of her flush and knew they'd be able to see the evidence of her embarrassment even in the dim light. She'd politely excused herself and they'd all chuckled as she'd scurried inside like the young naïve woman she'd been. But after she'd returned to the kitchen, she'd heard Kyle say, "Buddy, you are going to have to watch that one like a hawk. I know you consider her a sister so I'm just going to tell you straight up—she is so fucking smart and gorgeous,

I think it's going to take all of us to look after her."

Before that night, Jen had only heard a few rumblings about BDSM. But Kyle West's comment had sparked her interest. Could there be elements of the lifestyle that were more relationship oriented than she'd imagined? His words hadn't had any sexual connotations at all, but had sounded…almost protective. After that night she'd begun reading about BDSM clubs and the broad spectrum of elements related to those who enjoyed the lifestyle. There were several recurring themes, including the importance of communication and the fact that everything that happened had to be consensual. But the one element that stuck in her mind was a tenet one Dominant had written. He'd stated that his job as a Dom was to continually seduce submission from his sub and that providing for her, protecting her, and cherishing her were privileges not obligations.

After she'd learned those things, she'd seen the entire BDSM scene in a whole new light. Sure there were elements that scared the crap out of her and there were some things she knew she would never be able to even consider trying. *Nope, nobody is going to pee on me.* Jen had visited the Masters of the Prairie Winds website religiously, so she'd known every rule by heart before she'd been unceremoniously left in the Wests care after the disaster in Costa Rica last year.

Sighing to herself, Jen tried to refocus on the man sitting so patiently in front of her. He was studying her intently as if he could read her thoughts just by looking at her, and with his experience as a Dom perhaps he could. Each man in the room was watching her with the same intent expression…except Kent who seemed content, as if her acceptance was already in the bag. Shaking off her distraction, she asked, "Can you tell me specifically what you would be asking me to do? I want to make sure I'm really clear on what you're expecting...because, well frankly, your offer seems a little bit too good to be true."

For the first time since she'd returned to Prairie Winds a week ago, Jen saw Kyle West smile. She was taken aback momentarily at how much such a simple facial expression change could transpose the man's appearance. *Holy shit, he is absolutely stunning when he smiles. No wonder Tobi worships both brothers.* Jen had actually wondered on occasion why Tobi seemed so smitten with the more serious Kyle West. But when he smiled everything about him changed and as a student of body language the lesson wasn't lost on her. "I have to say, Jen, I am impressed with your wisdom. Asking for clarification before making any decision is only smart. But letting us all know up front that you see the offer as 'too good to be true' is a huge relief to all of us. I'm not going to lie, we want you on board. You have skills that will benefit our teams, we'll be counting on you to teach some of those skills to our current and future operatives as well. You are fearless and smart, and every member of the team likes and respects you. You'll be a very real asset to our team."

For some reason, Jen knew he'd stopped before he had actually told her everything, so she just waited. Watching him closely, she could see the barely detectable twitch of his jaw muscle. *Yep, there it is...that small, yet significant telltale sign that there is more to say and he was struggling to hold it back, unsure that voicing the thought is a good idea.* And in that instant her decision was made. They really could use her skills. Knowing what was going through a person's subconscious mind could easily mean the difference between life or death in the situations these men would be putting themselves in. She had used disguises before and she knew she could blend in regardless of the environment...hell, she'd essentially grown up doing that very thing. And with sudden clarity, Jen realized all of her experiences—both good and bad—in various foster homes were about to prove valuable. *Finally.*

Kyle's smile warmed to something that looked more like what she would expect from a friend, and Jen just continued to wait patiently. He finally chuckled and added, "And Kent and I will be very pleased that our *wife* will be pleased." Jen must have looked surprised because Kyle laughed out loud. "Don't look so shocked, Jen, Tobi may not be in the room, but I promise you she's definitely had a hand in the offer I just laid out for you. She was more than a little bit determined that you would join us. I've always despaired that so many people discount the intelligence of beautiful women, and one thing you need to know about Tobi is that she is drop-dead gorgeous *and* absolutely brilliant when it comes to marketing. She understands the importance of putting each one of a dozen different elements together in exactly the right combination to make something work, and that is one of the very basics of assembling an effective team."

Jen grinned and relaxed marginally for the first time since she'd entered the elegant room a half hour earlier. "I totally understand being underestimated based on appearance, and I wouldn't have made that judgment about Tobi because her intelligence shines brightly in her eyes. But I am surprised that she is so set on my joining the team. Can you tell me specifically why that is?" She saw Kyle's gaze flick behind her and when his eyes softened she knew Tobi had entered the room.

"I'll answer this one for myself if you don't mind, Kyle." Jen turned and greeted Tobi as she strode forward.

"There are a lot of reasons I'd like to see you on the team, including the fact I think we could be great friends and I'd like to see you living close. But the most important thing is, the type of work this team is considering is dangerous. Any edge they can get will keep them that much safer and your knowledge of verbal as well as non-verbal communication will be a huge asset to them. As Doms they read people extremely well within certain parameters, but not all of their missions will be in BDSM clubs..." Tobi gave a yelp as Kent landed a very solid sounding swat on Tobi's ass. "Damn—s and rivers. That hurt."

"And now you owe me another, sweetness. You know that cursing isn't allowed. We want to be sure you have broken the habit before the baby gets here." Kent turned to Jen, "And at the rate this is going, we don't stand a snow-ball's chance in hell of meeting that deadline. Now, I want to hear you accept our offer so I can get sweet mama here upstairs to rest."

Jen found herself laughing at their antics and as she turned back, Sam's gaze was full of hope and she wondered what affect her joining the team would have on their budding relationship. She looked to each of the men in the room and then asked, "Have you all discussed this? Is this something everyone agrees on? Because I don't want to become a part of a team if I'm not truly going to be included. I don't want to be just a token member."

Kyle snorted back a laugh, but it was Jax who an-swered, "Jen, we all agree that you'll be a very real asset to the team. I'm not saying we will always agree on exactly how that will play out each time we need your particular skill set, but I can promise you this—you will have an equal say in that decision making process. We won't treat you as anything less than a full member of the team, that is not how we operate."

Jen smiled and nodded, "Thanks, Jax, I appreciate the fact you will take my input seriously because if I'm not going to be a real member of the team, I wouldn't bother." Turning back to Kyle, she continued, "I'd be happy to join your team, Kyle. I'll need to contact my supervisor at the State Department and give my notice, but I'm actually on leave for the next three weeks so as soon as I can fly back to Washington and clean out my apartment I'll drive my car out here, find an apartment, and be ready to go to work."

Kyle stood and reached across to shake her hand, "You tender your resignation and let us figure out something with your car. Your apartment has already been cleaned and the few things that weren't destroyed have been shipped here and are waiting for you in the maintenance building. Personally, I'd rather you didn't return to Washington because the trip would cost me three members of my team, and since we've already been contacted about a job you will to be involved in, we'd prefer everybody was close for meetings. Also, let's not be hasty looking for an apartment." Kyle didn't elaborate but Jen was sure she understood what he meant, and the looks she was getting from Sam and Sage confirmed her suspicions.

Jen heard Tobi speaking behind her and turned just in time for her friend to step up and pull her into a crushing hug. "I'm so glad you'll be staying. We'll be having a girls' celebration at the gazebo at four o'clock this afternoon. It'll be fun and we'll gossip about the men. Don't be late or we'll send Lilly after you." Tobi was giggling as Kent shook his head and pulled her against his side before he ushered her out the door. For the first time in a long time, Jen felt like things were actually going her way. She was exploring her sexuality with the two men who had starred in every fantasy she'd had for the past year. She'd just landed a job that would not only offer her the chance to make the world a better place, but she'd be working with a great team. And the generous financial incentives meant she could start thinking about pursuing her PhD.

SAM HADN'T REALIZED how apprehensive he'd been about how Jen would respond to the job offer he'd known Kyle was going to present to her until she'd agreed to come on board. He'd taken a deep breath for the first time since they'd sat down when she and Kyle had shaken hands, feeling more relieved than he'd thought possible. He knew there would be a lot of hurdles to overcome, but she was one step closer to belonging to he and Sage, and right now that was all that mattered.

Kyle excused himself to go check on Tobi, and Jax and Micah said they planned to leave right away also. They were anxious to return home to check on Gracie and Jen hugged them both and smiled at the relief she saw in their eyes. Sam turned to Jen and smiled, "I'm not sure you know how pleased Sage and I are that you'll be staying here, Jen." He knew his use of her name had surprised her and he grinned. "When we're working we'll try to be as professional as possible and that means curbing the use of endearments. Although I want to go on record as saying I'm not going to spend a lot of time breaking the habit. I like thinking of you as *pet* and my *love* because that is the way my heart sees you. But neither Sage nor I want to undermine your position on the team so we'll try to be as professional as we can when we're all working."

Sage had stepped up along Jen's other side and grinned, "Well, we'd planned this elaborate scheme to convince you to accept Kent and Kyle's offer and now we find we have a few hours free before the ladies' soiree, so I was just wondering…" Jen started giggling and shaking her head at Sage's antics and Sam appreciated the fact his brother had lightened the moment, because the break had given him a chance to push back some of the emotion he was feeling. Hell, after spending the past decade working in every conceivable environment, you'd think he would be a master at pushing his personal feelings aside, but there was something about Jen that brought all those well practice defense mechanisms crashing down around him.

Jen's smile faded and she looked at them with sincerity, "Just remember, I want to earn my way on the team. I don't want anyone to think I'm only here because of the two of you. I don't want to be the girlfriend that got the job because of her boyfriends." *Because I'd most certainly lose it when things fold as they always do.*

"Not to worry because we intend to make sure you are fully prepared for everything this job will throw at you. Your life and the lives of each team member depends on it." Jen nodded and Sam continued speaking, but his words were directed to Sage even though he didn't take his eyes off hers, "Actually, I was thinking we should head down to the shooting range and make sure our new teammate is well versed in the weapons she'll be expected to use." He leaned forward and pressed his lips against her forehead, "What do you think? Wanna go shoot some paper?" He couldn't hold back his laugh when he saw the child-like enthusiasm and anticipation in her eyes. Jax had already warned them not to be taken in by her, that she was a crack shot and a hustler of the first order. They didn't care if she played them, they'd happily hand over the cash if it meant seeing her smile. *Oh yeah, McCall, you are so screwed.*

Chapter Twenty

WALKING INTO THE gazebo, Jen was shocked at the spread before her. *Easy to see the hostess is pregnant. Holy mother of mermaids that is a lot of food.* Lilly looked up and cackled with laughter. "Amazing isn't it? All afternoon Tobi has been adding food items and the cooks at the house have been frantically trying to keep up. One of them offered me money to take her out of the house and confiscate her phone."

"Well, if they'd let me inside the kitchen I could have helped. I'm not really quite as bad as everyone lets on I am...okay, that was a lie, but there are some things I can do." Tobi started giggling and Jen felt herself relaxing.

Gracie was sitting off to the side with a plate of crackers but for the first time since Jen had been back in Texas, the Latino beauty didn't look green. "Hey, Gracie, you look better. How are you feeling?"

"Oh, I'm much better now. Once we finally found the right combination of medicine and diet, I'm not nearly as sick as I was before. But I'm not planning to eat any of the stuff Tobi eats. I swear there isn't any justice at all, she eats crazy and nothing seems to upset her stomach. And I can look at something spicy and it's all over but the shouting as Lilly is so fond of saying."

Lilly looked over and smiled at Gracie, "I was like you, Gracie. Hell, I swore I was going to throw up those damned twins. Little tummy terrorists!"

"Regi's hot doctors helped me so much. I am very thankful they live close." The sincerity of Gracie's words was easy to hear and Jen was glad her new friend had obstetricians she liked.

"Hey, they don't belong to me. Don't you be putting that idea in everybody's head. Damn, ya'all get knocked up and you want everybody to jump in the quicksand with you. Well don't be trying to pull me into the married and prego pit. I know you all are fooled by them, but let me tell you, I have their numbers. Tall, Dark, and Handsome Dr. McDreamy is more like Dr. Jekyll in the way he seems to be able to read your thoughts like they were written on your forehead." And then shaking her finger at Gracie, Regi plunged ahead, "And your knight in shining armor, Doc Hollywood, is more like Dr. Frankenstein considering his obsession with laser wands." Regi had shuddered and then, as if speaking to herself, she added softy, "Hell, it was a wonder my hair didn't look like a Brill-O pad after the last time I agreed to his little 'lights and magic show'." Everybody laughed at Regi's remarks, but it was obvious to Jen that Regi had been uncomfortable with the direction the conversation had been heading, so she'd used humor as a detour. What puzzled Jen the most was Regi's apparent discomfort with her own attraction to the good docs. *Interesting. I wonder what demons she is battling because those men are great looking, successful, and from what I've heard, they dote on her?* Jen had never been into the whole *girlfriends thing* because she'd been moved from one home to another so often during her early teens that she'd never gotten a chance to form those bonds, but for the first time ever she could see herself enjoying the camaraderie and friendship of other women.

Everyone loaded their plate and sat around the fire pit that proudly displayed the unique Prairie Winds logo around the sides. The conversation was light as they enjoyed the fire's warmth and softly glowing ambiance. The flickering light added a sense of coziness and watching the dancing flames was almost hypnotizing. Jen watched as Lilly mothered both Tobi and Gracie, tending to their every whim despite their continued protests that they were just pregnant, not invalids. It was just entering Jen's mind that the West brother's vivacious mother always seemed to return to her seat and carefully slid beneath a small lap quilt that seemed oddly out of place when she heard the snapping of twigs behind her.

Between one breath and the next, Jen felt as if the whole world had shifted. Gracie paled as if she'd seen a ghost, Tobi's breath caught and the expletives she uttered would have made a sailor blush, and Lilly's hand stealthfully slid beneath the quilt despite the fact her eyes were fixed over Jen's right shoulder. "Well, well, God certainly is smiling on me tonight because both of my women are in one place. This will make things so much easier." Jen didn't have to turn around to know the man speaking was Raphael Baldamino, his accent placed his home along the Pacific coast of Central America and Gracie's reaction had sealed the deal.

When she shifted in her seat to face him, she was surprised to find he was already standing close enough to run his hand over her shoulder and then back up so it was wrapped around her neck. The gesture was an odd mix of intimacy and power as he tightened his grip around her throat in a show of strength even as his thumb massaged gentle circles along the hairline at the back of her skull. She looked at him and felt the anger pulsing from him. Jen had seen pictures of Baldamino and knew he'd been a handsome man before the helicopter crash, and she'd been told that he'd always taken great pride in his appearance. But now, the man he'd been was barely recognizable. The scarring from the burns he'd suffered were horrible and she wondered why a man as wealthy as he was hadn't received the best medical treatment money could buy. Then it dawned on her, he wouldn't have been able to seek that treatment without disclosing the fact he'd survived the explosion everyone had assumed had claimed everyone on board.

"Don't move, Daisy." His voice was raspy and Jen froze because for just a second she'd been unsure exactly who he was speaking to. *Daisy? Who the hell is Daisy?* "You'll be the perfect balance to my Rose over there. You'll be the lovely *light* to her delicious *dark* beauty and with the two of you on my arm no one will notice the scars I carry." *Oh, I'm willing to bet your shiny new coat of crazy is still going to show...a lot! And he's decided to call me Daisy? Like that chic with the short shorts on the Dukes of Hazard? Nope, I don't think that is gonna work for me. Asshat.*

Lilly West started to stand and the King of the Loonies snarled at her, "Don't move, Mrs. West. You have already caused me enough trouble. What the hell did you shoot at that boat anyway, a fucking bazooka? I swear, woman, you have some sort of Annie Oakley complex. I should shoot your damned husbands for allowing you to even own a firearm. I have no clue what might have possessed them to think *that* was a good idea. They really appear to be intelligent businessmen, but fuck me—putting a gun in your hands is just plain irresponsible."

Jen felt his grip tighten around her throat and felt herself sway. She could see the fire flash in Lilly's eyes and even though she didn't know the woman particularly well, everything about her body language screamed a warning that her response to the jackass gripping Jen's throat was not going to play out well for anyone. Lilly tilted her chin and gave him what Jen knew was likely a well-honed look of haughty indifference. "Well, I'm not sure who you are, but you seem to know everyone here so perhaps you'd like to introduce yourself." *Good plan, Lilly. Stall. The men have to know by now there is a problem.* She'd seen Tobi move her fingers over the cuff bracelet she wore all the time and knew she had pressed the panic button that was disguised as one of the sparkling gemstones.

Tobi and Gracie both wore jewelry that allowed the Prairie Winds security team to know their location at any given moment. The pieces also gave the women the opportunity to activate an alarm in case they needed help. Tobi had done a good job of making her motions look like nothing more than nervous fidgeting, but Jen hadn't been fooled. Baldamino snorted in disgust before looking at Lilly as if she was nothing more than a bothersome pest. "Don't play coy, Mrs. West. My name is Raphael Baldamino and I am not interested in playing your social games. Buying time is not going to help you, I'm taking Rose and Daisy with me back to Costa Rica and it is time for us to go." Jerking Jen to her feet, he moved his bruising grip to her upper arm and she winced when he clamped down on her tender flesh. Taking two steps toward Gracie, Jen saw Jax and Micah's wife start to shake in fear just before her entire demeanor changed and she tilted her chin in defiance.

Gracie looked up at him and snarled, "I'm not going anywhere with you. Let go of Jen. You are hurting her. Why do you feel you should be allowed to just take whatever you decide is yours even when it clearly is not?"

Jen saw him raise his other hand, the glint of light off metal confirmed her worst fear…he was armed. When he raised his arm and pointed the gun at Lilly, Jen felt herself sway and in the next instant she saw Lilly's hand raise with a weapon of her own. Lilly's eyes met Jen's for just the briefest of seconds before they flickered toward the floor, but it was enough for Jen to know exactly what she was supposed to do.

With every bit of drama she could manage, Jen swayed again and starting to shake and then dropped like a stone. Before she'd hit the floor Jen heard two deafening cracks as both weapons were fired almost simultaneously. Baldamino's lifeless body slumped over her and she felt the sticky warmth of blood before he rolled to the floor with a sickening thud. Her ears were ringing because the man's hand had been so close to her head when he'd fired his weapon but she could hear Gracie's scream over Lilly's cursing. And it registered in her mind that if Lilly was cursing at least she was alive.

The pounding of boots on the wooden deck of the gazebo brought her attention to the men swarming them but Jen's gaze sought out Sam and Sage and never wavered from them until Sage's arms wrapped around her. She felt herself being lifted from the floor and heard him asking her if she was all right, but as much as she wanted to tell him the blood wasn't hers, she couldn't form the words and then everything faded very slowly to black.

SAM AND SAGE had been walking in the back door of the club when they'd nearly been run over by several members of the security team. The quick jerk of Kent's head had the two of them following as he'd asked Micah who was in the control center. The life of every Special Forces soldier is continually balanced along a razor's edge and often the only thing standing between the team and death is their communications officer. So finding out who was handing logistics and communication was as natural as breathing in a crisis situation. Micah's terse, "Ash" was answer enough. Even though Sam had never been a teammate of Ash's, his skills were well known and respected among the other squads. It was Micah's next words that sent a chill through Sam's blood, "Baldamino is in the gazebo with the girls."

"How?" Sam had barely been able to choke out the word as an unfamiliar wave of fear washed over him.

"Looks like he stole Dean and Dell's boat so nobody noticed when it docked. The system is set up to recognize the digital signals of certain vessels, so their boat didn't attract any attention." The frustration in Micah's voice was easy to hear. Sam knew without question that *hole* in their system would be addressed immediately. But right now their priority was getting the women away from Baldamino. As they ran down the cobblestone path leading to the gazebo every possible scenario ran through Sam's mind and too many of those didn't end well. Just as they rounded the last curve in the shrub lined path two shots rang out and Sam felt like he'd been gut punched.

SAGE SPRINTED AHEAD of everyone and into the gazebo just in time to see Baldamino's body roll off Jen. He was grateful for all his years of training or he wasn't sure how he would have reacted to the blood covering her back. She looked up from her crouched position and he saw her frantic search of the men entering the white wooden structure until she found him and Sam. Her gaze never wavered as he quickly made his way to her and pulled her up into his arms. Putting even the smallest of distances between them so he could ask her if she was hurt, was excruciating. He'd picked her up and looked into her sweet face and watched as her eyes seem to dull and lose focus just before they rolled back and she went limp in his arms.

Sage looked on as Sam had leaned down to check the man laying at his feet, but it hadn't been necessary, the single bullet hole in the middle of his scarred face had told them everything they had needed to know. Sage laid Jen on one of the tables and he and Sam quickly checked to be sure the only blood on her wasn't actually hers. Once they were sure she wasn't injured Sam had picked her up and headed to their cabin to get her cleaned up while Sage stayed and helped sort through what had happened.

Lilly was cursing like a sailor about the fact Baldamino had winged her before she'd taken him out, and both Kent and Kyle looked like they were about ready to blow a gasket. Tobi was leaning over her mother-in-law wrapping the wound in a cloth napkin and Sage could hear sirens in the distance. Lilly's voice had taken on the distinct *mother-tone* that all kids recognize and Sage had to bite back his smile. "Stop barking at me, Kyle West. I'm already about five shades of pissed off and I don't need you telling me I should have waited for you and your brother to get here. Hell, I wasn't going to let him take Gracie and Jen. And he didn't seem like he was exactly the president of my fan club either. Besides...he pointed his gun at me, so I am perfectly within my rights to defend myself and others. Look it up." Then she'd muttered something that made Tobi snort a quick laugh but Sage hadn't been able to catch it all, but it was clear she hadn't been at all pleased about being called Annie Oakley either.

"You know the dads are going to be pissed that you brought a gun to the party, right? What exactly were you thinking?" Kyle had begun pacing in front of his wife and mother and Sage could see he was struggling to hold on to his patience. Sage had seen it a thousand times, Kyle was lashing out because he felt out of control and from the look on Lilly's face, she was also fast approaching the end of her rope.

"What was I thinking? I was thinking I might have to use it. Why else does anyone carry a weapon? Geez, Kyle, that wasn't a very smart question. You can do better than that." For the first time he heard Lilly's voice relax a bit and he was glad she seemed to be calming down, even if it was only fractionally. And then she looked up and Sage got a brief glimpse of a much wilder and much younger Lilly West as she grinned and added, "I wasn't looking for trouble, but you have to admit, I hang out with a rough crowd." Tobi and Gracie both stared at her, their mouths gapping open, until they both dissolved into hysterical laughter. Lilly's sly grin showed how pleased she was that her attempt to distract Kyle had been successful and the tension drained from Kent as well. Emergency personnel from several different agencies stormed them and Sage slipped away and headed for the cabin to check on Jen.

Sage knew they'd have to take her back up to the gazebo to answer questions, but they'd wanted to get that asshole's blood off her as soon as possible and he was anxious to see how she was coping. Not everyone would deal well with having a dead man collapse over them. Personally, he was thrilled that Lilly West had taken care of the insane prick who terrorized Gracie and Jen. Raphael

Baldamino wouldn't be a problem for either of them ever again. And even though there would be a hundred men and women who would be more than happy to fill his shoes in Central America's underworld, at least the momentum of growth Baldamino had achieved would be slowed for a while and his predecessors wouldn't share his obsession with Jen and Gracie.

Knowing the team the Wests were in the process of bringing together would now have time to properly train to work together helped ease Sage's mind. He and Sam had been conflicted about bringing Jen on board, but in the end, having her in danger where they could help was better than having her unprotected and attracting trouble while working for the State Department. The general consensus was that someone in her agency had sold her out to Baldamino, and if it happened once it would certainly happen again. Sage knew there were efforts being made already to figure out who was responsible and then they would be able to put together a plan to deal with the culprit—he and Sam both had some very strong ideas about how that should play out, but it was likely the Wests would hand over the traitor to the authorities.

Pausing for a moment on the cabin's large front porch, Sage took a deep breath and sent up a prayer of thanks to the Universe for sending them Jen and for protecting her once again. It didn't matter how long it took—he and Sam would make her theirs. Smiling to himself, he shook his head as he thought back on everything that had happened in the past year and remembered Dean West's advice.

He'd been standing on the curb in front of the hotel the morning after Jax, Gracie, and Micah's wedding celebration waiting for the valet to bring his truck around when he'd noticed the elder West standing to his side. Jen had pulled a disappearing act sometime during the very early hours of the morning, and he and Sam had been livid that she managed to give them the slip. In truth, Sage had been devastated she'd felt the need to escape them.

Dean West had looked at him and smiled, "I know you aren't happy with how this has played out, Sage. But I want you to consider this, would you be attracted to a woman who wasn't filled with fire? Would a woman who didn't challenge you light up yours and Sam's life?" He paused for just a moment, giving Sage the time to consider the question, and then continued, "It is only the strong ones that can survive a polyamorous relationship because there are tremendous social pressures that come into play...things the men in a relationship rarely have to face, but the women face regularly." Sage considered Dean's words and then nodded. "There are a lot of judgmental people out there and they only see love as acceptable if it falls within their very narrow parameters. They won't often express those bits of hate and discontent to you or Sam—they'll go after Jen. Now, I don't know that young lady well, but I can tell you she didn't run because she is weak. She ran because she has lost so much during her short life and I imagine the idea of losing you now feels safer to her than losing you after she gets in any deeper, because anybody watching the three of you can plainly see where her heart is."

Dean's words had surprised him and for several seconds Sage just stood staring at him. For the first time since he'd awakened to find Jen missing from their bed, he'd felt hopeful they hadn't lost her forever. He'd smiled at Dean and thanked him. When he'd reached forward to shake the man's hand, Dean had pulled him into a hug and said, "You two get yourselves safely back to Texas soon, you hear?" And then he'd strolled away. Sage had climbed in the truck just as Sam had walked out of the hotel and climbed in. After he'd told his brother about his encounter with Dean, the tension had drained from his brother as well.

Sage shook off the memories and walked into the

house just in time to hear Sam speaking to Jen, "Sexual awareness isn't a destination, Jen, it's a journey. And the path isn't a straight ribbon of highway curving across the west Texas prairie—rather it is a twisting, turning, switchback that meanders through the mountains and valleys. But the question is, are you really ready for the trip? Because unless you are ready to be completely honest with us and yourself, you aren't prepared for everything the trip has to offer and all the beautiful scenery will be wasted. You have to go in with your eyes and your heart open or all you'll see are the trees blocking your view along your way."

Stepping up alongside his brother, Sage felt his heart squeeze when he looked into her beautiful blue eyes. Their sapphire depths held his future and the significance of the moment was almost overwhelming in its intensity. Cupping the side of her face, he let the wet strands of her hair move over his fingers as he brushed the pad of his thumb over her flushed cheek. "We want you to focus on the forest, baby, not the trees. I'm not saying everything will be perfect, because you know none of us can make that promise. But I can tell you we'll always be here for you. There won't be a moment that we won't have your best interests at heart. We'd love nothing more than to show you all the ways there are to love, but you have to be willing to take a few risks. Are you willing to try?"

Her quick nod was all it took and their lives were changed in ways that only the future would reveal. But for this brief moment, everything was perfect. And the woman standing in front of them held their hearts in her hands.

Chapter Twenty-One

Four months later...

J EN STROLLED ALONG the pristine white beach of Boracay in the Philippines. With her sandals dangling from her fingers, she listened to the sounds of the never-ending party further up the beach and thought back at how very similar today was to the day her world had changed so dramatically. Oh, the location might be on the other side of the planet, but she could still feel the heartbeat of the ocean as if her body was synchronizing with its rhythm. *It feels so similar yet so much is different.* That day she'd been blissfully unaware of the fact she'd come to the attention of a monster. But her "almost" brother had already set plans in motion to whisk her out of harm's way, despite the fact she'd been seventeen hundred miles away. The men whose help he'd enlisted had turned her life upside down and stolen her heart. Knowing they were watching her now made her smile as she stepped into the foaming surf at the water's edge. There wasn't anything quite like feeling the warm sand beneath your feet as you let the steady beat of the ocean's waves bring everything back into synch.

After Raphael Baldamino's death, there had been a mad scramble to take over his various business ventures. Only one of those endeavors was of interest to the new Black Ops team Jen was working with. The Wests along with Jax and Micah's security business had joined forces and their teams were contracting with various government agencies and corporations. They would be specializing in hostage rescues and curbing the growing problem of the lucrative sex slave trade industry.

Recently there had been numerous abductions of women matching Jen's description from beaches just like this one. All the Intel they'd gathered indicated the current global market for sex trading was spiking in this part of the world...so here she was listening to the men chatter over her ear bud and making a heroic effort not to react. *And don't forget, walking along a beach alone smiling like a loon and chatting away at people no one else could see tends to make people think they should drop a net over you. And even though I don't have much experience with the finer details related to sex trafficking, I'm pretty sure insanity is not high on purchasers list of favored attributes.*

The past four months had been filled with intense training and more than once Jen had been certain she'd reached her limit. However, Sam and Sage had always encouraged her and she'd soon discovered her limits were far beyond anything she could have imagined. The information end of the training had been intense and challenging, but the physical part had been downright grueling. She'd had aches and pains in places she didn't even know she had and after the guerrilla-warrior brigade was finished with her, they'd turned her over to the preggo battalion yoga group to finish her off. Tobi West was a slave driver of biblical proportions and Jen wondered if the tiny tornado would actually rock that baby she was carrying or if she'd have the tyke down in the Prairie Winds gym working out every afternoon because "naps are for wimps". Jen and Lilly had "skipped class" one afternoon and hidden down at the boat dock, but Tobi and Gracie had found them and dragged them back to the gym.

Sage's voice came over her ear bud and Jen had to suppress her body's startle reflex. "I don't know, brother, our woman looks so beautiful standing at the edge of the surf—lost in thought. I'll bet we could get her to agree to marry us before we return home. The great thing is she can't talk back right now, oh yeah, this is a sweet arrangement indeed."

Not likely, lover boy. I already told you I want to be romanced and—

Sam interrupted her thoughts, "I don't know. I think our mom and sisters have already gotten to her. We'll probably have to grovel or do something ultra-romantic." Jen could hear the amusement in Sam's voice and found herself kicking at the waves so her smile didn't look so out of place. She stroked the soft feather she'd found while walking along the beach and smiled at the comfort it brought her. Millie Sinclair had been her last foster mother and the sweet woman had always reminded her that finding a feather was a reminder from heaven that someone she loved was watching over her from the other side. One of the last times Jen had spoken with Millie, they'd been sitting on the front porch swing and Millie had said, "Jen, you need to remember to fill your life with adventures. Anybody can muddle through, but it takes somebody with a real purpose in life to see all the opportunities for doing something special. You watch for those feathers and when you find them you'll know you are on the right path." In the weeks following Millie's sudden passing, Jen had found dozens of feathers. Some had been in such unlikely places Jen had laughed, knowing Millie was letting her know she was still close. Those feathers had brought her enormous comfort and had gotten Jen through many lonely nights.

Indeed your mom and sisters did have a long chat with me and you have no idea how disappointed they would be if they didn't get to see you get married. And I'm not starting off on the wrong side of the women in your family...nope, not happening. Jen didn't actually care how they ended up married, but she had really liked Sam and Sage's family, and if it was important to them to be a part of the wedding then it was important to Jen.

Sage groaned, "I'm not sure how we're going to pull off any romance in light of the fact there are so many eyes on her."

"And the real challenge is not all of them belong to us or our team. Head's up, everybody, we have incoming at three o'clock. Jen, don't look now but you have company on the way. Everybody else, focus. Both of these asshats are high on our watch list. I do believe it is show time people." Sam's voice had gone from fun to all business in the blink of an eye. Jen could almost feel her heart pounding in her chest and she was making a concentrated effort to keep her body language relaxed, after all she was just a young American woman on vacation.

She had every faith in her team, they weren't going to let anything happen to her and she'd been well trained for this moment. *Smile. Engage. Flirt. Question. Entrap.*

"Well, hi there, pretty lady. You look lonely. Would you like some company?" When she turned toward them she wanted to shudder. They were dressed in what she'd come to refer to as the uniform of the Indonesian underground. Khaki slacks and white cotton oxford shirts seemed to be the preferred wardrobe choice, but at least they blended in better than the all black outfits of the jerks she'd dealt with in Costa Rica.

"Oh, hi. Well, I'm not really lonely, but I'm always up for meeting new people. I was just enjoying a bit of beach time before I return home in a few days." The plan had been to make sure they knew she was leaving in a couple of days so they'd have to make a move quickly, since they wouldn't have long before she'd be missed.

"Where's home?"

The taller of the two seemed to be taking the lead so she directed her response to him, "Well, I'm not sure I should be giving out personal information to strangers." When he stepped forward, grasped her hand, and lifted it to his lips, kissing the back in a gesture that sent her stomach into a free-fall, she actually heard Sam growl. To calm her nerves, Jen concentrated on the fact she was wearing multiple tracking devices and was also transmitting their conversation to every man watching.

"Perhaps you'd like to share a drink with us and we could get to know each other better. We're staying at same hotel you are." She raised her brow in question and he smiled, "We have seen you the past couple of days and were just too shy to approach you." *Yeah, right, Fred. More like you were watching to see if I was staying alone. And I'll bet you have been through my room with a fine-toothed comb too.* She knew her room had been searched because she'd made sure to set enough little traps there was no way anyone could have noticed them all. It was amazing how effective a little bit of transparent tape and fishing line could be to let you know if anyone opened a door or drawer.

"I don't know. That doesn't sound like a very good idea, my friends warned me to not go off with strangers when traveling alone." She paused and looked at the sand dragging her toes through the soft sand. "Shoot, I shouldn't have said that."

"It's alright. We'll just walk you right up to the hotel and get acquainted." When they each grasped one of her arms just above her elbow she dug in her heels and started protesting their manhandling. "Keep quiet, Jennifer, and you won't get hurt. We have someone for you to meet and he'd prefer to speak with you when you can understand the offer he wants to make you. But we will get you there one way or another. And there isn't a single person on this beach who will interfere because they know who we work for."

"Wait. How did you know my name? And who do you work for?"

"Our leader is not from here, but you are in luck that Mr. Mendoza is in town visiting friends. He saw you on the street and wants to meet you. He has a beautiful suite at the hotel, I think you'll enjoy staying there." Staying there? Oh brother, if she was really traveling on her own, those words would have scared the daylights out of her. Who was she kidding? They scared her and she knew her backup was eyes on and would be pulling her out any minute. Their hands tightened with a vise-like grip on her upper arms and she wanted to kick them both for the bruises she was sure to have for the next several days.

"Well, if he's such a great guy, why did he send you to fetch me like a bone for a dog? And you lied to me about wanting to get to know me, so I think I'll decline your invitation. Let me go or I'm going to make a big scene." They'd both just laughed and lifted her so her feet were barely touching the ground. Knowing Roberto Mendoza was staying in the same hotel where she'd been sleeping was disconcerting to say the least. Mendoza was pure evil wrapped in a deceptively attractive and charming package.

When she looked ahead and saw Sage ambling along casually with a beach towel draped over his arm she felt a wave of relief. Dex Raines and Ash Moore were to his left and each of them had their hands shoved into the pockets of their cargo shorts and were no doubt gripping their weapons just as she knew Sage was. And even though she'd known they were watching and listening, it was altogether different when she could actually see her teammates.

She struggled in their hold so anyone they met would have a perfectly good reason to inquire about her well-being and Sage played his part beautifully. "Hey, Jen, wasn't it? We met on the plane, do you remember? I was telling my friends about you and we'd wondered where you were staying. We're having a little get together tonight here on the beach if you are interested." When the men didn't stop she looked up and knew the frantic expression on her face wasn't all acting. "Hey, hold up, guys. We want to talk to the lady." When the three of them blocked their path, the men stopped but didn't make any attempt to let her go. Sage's eyes went to where their hands were encircled around her arm and frowned. "Are you okay, darlin'? Because you don't seem very happy and I'm not overly thrilled with the way this looks."

"She is fine. She is on her way to a business meeting and is going to be late. We must go now." When they tried to push past the three former SEALs, Jen watched as Dex and Ash each moved with lightning speed pressing on the men's wrists causing them to release her into Sage's waiting arms. They had the two cuffed and were quietly escorting them up the beach before most of the other tourists had even realized what had happened right in front of them.

Jen was grateful Sage kept his arm wrapped tightly around her, securely anchoring her against his side. His presence made her feel grounded and safe, and it terrified her to realize how quickly women were overpowered and whisked away never to be seen again. And for the first time she understood how easily she could have become just another victim in Costa Rica. Knowing how close she'd come to never seeing any of her friends again was almost too much to deal with. When they reached the street the men were handed over to the authorities and Sage turned her so she was facing him. She looked up into his eyes and saw all the love and protectiveness she'd always yearned for reflected back at her. He pulled her into his arms and just held her, not saying anything for several minutes, and she wasn't sure which of them was more comforted by the gesture.

When he finally released her, he brushed her hair back behind her ear and cupped the side of her face, "Are you okay, baby?" Jen knew both Sage and Sam had been working hard to keep their promise and they'd actually done a great job of keeping their use of endearments out of their work environment. But right now she found his words enormously comforting and she didn't mind at all. When she merely nodded he smiled, "You were fucking amazing. We got everything. Mendoza's suite is being raided as we speak. Your things are already in the truck, we didn't want to risk you returning for them. We'll turn over copies of the tapes to the task force and be on a plane before dark."

Just as Sage finished speaking, a large black SUV pulled up and Sam leapt from the passenger's side before it had even stopped moving. He strode toward her with a predator's grace and determination. When his eyes moved over her, Jen could tell the instant he noticed the marks on her biceps. He didn't stop until he was close enough that she could feel the heat from his body and that sensation had no sooner registered than he slammed his mouth down on hers in a kiss she knew was purely adrenaline driven. By the time he released her they were both panting and she felt her pussy flooding with desire. *Holy shit, that adrenaline is powerful stuff.* She hadn't realized how pumped she was until Sam had kissed her and she'd practically crawled up his body like a spider monkey. Neither Sam nor Sage said another word, they simply turned, and in five seconds they were all three in the back seat and speeding down the street.

JEN CAME AWAKE slowly, unsure about the engine noise she was hearing until she remembered boarding the Wests' private jet. She had answered questions until she'd been utterly exhausted and even though she'd been hungry, she simply hadn't been able to stay awake long enough to eat once they'd been in the air. Throwing back the cover, she made her way into the small bathroom and by the time she reemerged a few minutes later she felt much better, but her stomach was demanding to be fed so she opened the door into the main cabin.

She heard Sam's voice and turned toward him, but he had his back to her. She heard him speaking and knew immediately he was talking to his mother. Susie McCall was a force to be reckoned with and Jen had liked her immediately. "I understand and Sage and I are giving you two weeks to get it together." His exasperated sigh made Jen smile, he was clearly not pleased with whatever his mom had to say. "Three weeks. Final offer, Mom. Take it or we'll make a detour to Hawaii and be married before we hit the mainland." She saw his shoulders relax and knew his negotiation had been successful. When he spoke again, his tone was much softer and Jen could hear the love reflected in his words, "I want you to be happy but, Mom, Jen is ours and we want to start our lives with her. She is everything Sage and I have always dreamed of and we don't want to wait any longer to make her our wife." It was only then that she realized he'd been able to see her reflection in the window he was facing. He'd known all along she was there and when she stepped up behind him and wrapped her arms around his waist, he pulled her around and wrapped his arm around her. "Yes, Mom, I agree, she is absolutely perfect, well except for her tendency to eavesdrop, but I think we'll be able to handle that." Jen could hear his mom's cackle of laughter as they said their goodbyes and Sam tossed his phone into a nearby seat.

For the first time, Jen realized she felt like she fully *belonged*, and the feeling had been completely natural. She hadn't had to continually remind herself that she was worthy of the opportunity in front of her and the feeling made her almost giddy. The warmth of Sam's embrace doubled when she felt Sage press himself against her back. She felt safe and loved for the first time since Millie died and the significance of the journey she'd been on wasn't lost on her. Millie had always reminded her to look forward rather than back. Millie's determined voice floated through her mind, "You don't walk backwards through life, Jen, so there is no reason for you to always be looking that direction. You keep looking back and you'll miss a lot of the great things along life's path." Jen sent up a silent prayer of thanks for the woman who had made such an incredible difference in her life. *I never got to tell you what a profound difference you made in my life. But I promise to try to make a positive difference in as many lives as I can...that will be my way of saying thanks.* When Sam stepped back, Jen looked around the beautiful jet and her eyes locked on a small painting near the exit. She felt her heart pounding as she looked at the small oil painting of a perfect white feather that looked as if it was floating on a soft breeze against a blue summer sky. She hoped Susie McCall could manage the three-week deadline, because Jen had just gotten Millie's blessing and now she couldn't wait for her next adventure to begin.

Epilogue

Two weeks and five days later…

"LEAVE IT TO our mother and sisters to push the deadline until you could almost see the calendar stretching to accommodate them." Sam was pacing the room as Sage stood looking out over the elaborate setup in the backyard of their parents' home. "Honestly, we should have just stopped and gotten married in Hawaii. I should have never given mom a chance to pull this together. Hell, who on earth besides Susie McCall can manage to organize something of this scale in such a ridiculously short time." Sage couldn't remember ever seeing Sam this rattled, but he wasn't going to jump on the crazy-train either. Sage much preferred to have his head in exactly the right place.

Just as Sage was about to tell his older brother to chill there was a soft knock on the door. Sage pulled the door open and was shocked to see Jen standing in the hall looking absolutely terrified. "Baby? What's wrong?" He pulled her in to the room and closed the door behind her, if his mother or sisters got wind that they'd seen her in her wedding dress before the ceremony there would be hell to pay.

She didn't answer for several seconds and Sage was starting to worry. When he looked up at his brother his worry shifted to Sam because he looked as if he was about ready to have a stroke. *Christ, what is the problem with these two? This is supposed to be the happiest day of their lives and they are both about to jump out of their skin.* Jen finally took a deep breath and then focused her gaze on the floor as she whispered, "I was freaking out…and I…well, I just needed to see you. You balance me. Your touch grounds me and I needed that. And there are so many people out there and I only know about ten of them." Her voice had started to vibrate with fear and Sage found himself agreeing with Sam, they should have eloped and just suffered the consequences. It had never occurred to him how intimidated she might be by the scale of the celebration their family had planned. Actually, this was so typical of his mother and sisters; neither he nor Sam had found it unusual and that oversight was something he now regretted.

Sam stepped forward and grasped her hands and frowned. "Good God, love. Your hands are like ice. Come here." He pulled her toward the small sofa facing the stone fireplace and settled her on his knees facing Sage. Sam leaned forward and kissed the tip of her nose, mindful of her make-up, and then grinned. "You look amazing by the way. And we swear too never tell the McCall women that we saw you before the ceremony."

"Oh shit. I forgot about that. Frack me." When they both laughed she grinned, "I promised Tobi I'd do the no cursing thing with her. Kyle and Kent are threatening her with all sorts of bizarre punishments if she curses in front of the baby, so I thought maybe the buddy system would help her out. But so far, I'm the only one making any progress. Personally, I think it's a lost cause." Sage laughed and leaned forward gently rubbed his nose against hers.

"I'm glad you seem to be more relaxed, baby. And I'm sorry everything has gotten out of hand. I'm not going to lie to you, this is exactly the sort of thing that will happen anytime we let our mother or sisters take over the planning of any event. My suggestion is that you just learn to roll with it...Sam and I have found life is much less stressful that way." They spent a few more minutes enjoying the quiet before there was another knock at the door.

When Kyle West entered he smiled when he saw Jen, "I'm glad you're here, Jen, even if I'm going to have to pretend I didn't see you." His expression became more serious as he focused his attention on the men, "We have a situation developing and it's in the same location as your honeymoon plans." His eyes flicked to Jen and then back at the men. She'd been trying to get them to tell her where they were going for the past two weeks and obviously Kyle knew that. *Damn, I'll bet everybody knows but me. Which explains why they have been keeping Tobi from me today.* The men continued talking and agreed to keep in touch with Kyle in case there was any way for the three of them to help since they'd be close. Just as they were finishing up, the door swung open and Susie McCall stormed into the room. *Well fuck a fat fairy in a fur coat. We are so busted.*

REGI LOOKED IN the full-length mirror and frowned. *What on earth was I thinking?* With Gracie and Tobi both declining Jen's request for the three of them to be bridesmaids, Regi hadn't felt like she could let their friend down by being the third strike. But now that she saw what an enormous production the whole thing was, she was more than a little bit worried. It turns out the McCalls were among the moneyed one percent and their sons' wedding was making the news in a lot of ways. The chances of some photographer snapping her picture was huge and if there was one thing she did not need, it was having her picture plastered in the society pages for every two bit thug wanting to make points with "the family" to see. She could only hope the hair and make-up artists Susie McCall hired had done their job so she wouldn't be recognized.

Taking a deep breath, she turned away from the mirror and tried to push her worries to the back of her mind. There were more pressing things to worry about right now...namely the two handsome doctors who would be escorting her this evening. *Talk about having a dim moment...I have no idea what possessed me to think I could handle them on top of everything else tonight.* She laughed to herself as she descended the stairs into the chaos—possessed was probably more accurate than she cared to admit.

The End

Books by Avery Gale

The Wolf Pack Series
Mated – Book One
Fated Magic – Book Two
Tempted by Darkness – Book Three

Masters of the Prairie Winds Club
Out of the Storm
Saving Grace
Jen's Journey
Bound Treasure
Punishing for Pleasure
Accidental Trifecta
Missionary Position

The ShadowDance Club
Katarina's Return – Book One
Jenna's Submission – Book Two
Rissa's Recovery – Book Three
Trace & Tori – Book Four
Reborn as Bree – Book Five
Red Clouds Dancing – Book Six
Perfect Picture – Book Seven

Club Isola

Capturing Callie – Book One

Healing Holly – Book Two

Claiming Abby – Book Three

I would love to hear from you!

Email:

avery.gale@ymail.com

Website:

www.averygalebooks.com/index.html

Facebook:

facebook.com/avery.gale.3

Instagram:

avery.gale

Twitter:

@avery_gale

Excerpt from Fated Magic

The Wolf Pack
Book Two
by Avery Gale

KIT PACED THE length of her husbands' office like a caged animal during the entire meeting regarding the boy her mother simply referred to as Braden. Jameson hadn't hesitated a moment in his agreement to take the teenager in and the rest of the meeting had been taken up with logistics and planning for his safety as well as the safety of everyone else living at the estate. Kit was in favor of taking him in and knew her friend well enough to know where he'd be staying once he arrived. It was obvious that Angie had felt a very real connection to the young man and Kit was relieved that everyone was rallying around him. Her restlessness had nothing to do with Braden...no her frustration was directed entirely at her two Alpha mates.

Trying to tell me that I have to wait for the next full moon to run. Damn wolves think they can rule the world just because they are the Alphas of the pack. Don't think so, fellas, I am running tonight if I have to leap out of a damned window naked and fly into the forest on a damned broom. She'd always detested the image of witches on brooms because it was about the most ridiculous bit of imagination in history if you asked Kit.

Brooms? Really? Like any self-respecting witch needed a damned broom.

Spending the past four months cooped up in the estate was taking a toll on her sanity and if she didn't get out soon she was going to be a loon. At first she'd been too busy with the babies to worry about the fact she often spent the entire day in her pajamas. But the only thing that had kept a lid on her growing frustration was the fact she'd been spending a lot of quality time in the gym expending copious amounts of energy in every sort of physical outlet she could find. Well, all but the one she wanted to be enjoying. Her husbands had, for some reason, decided vanilla sex was more acceptable for a "mother" and she was seriously considering drowning them both.

How can anyone who can be replaced by a battery-operated device consider himself the Lord and Master of his Kingdom? I didn't even get a honeymoon. Nope I went straight from caught to mated to knocked up. Once they got what they wanted all was well in the Wolf brothers little Alpha paradise. Whoever decided men should be the leaders of a pack or any other group really needed to study ancient history. Fat fairies will fly over Philly before I settle for vanilla sex for the rest of my life. It's just mean. Show me all the fun of kink and then take it away? I don't fucking think so.

She'd finally received the go-ahead from the doctors to shift and run tonight and then Jameson had "suggested" that she wait until the next full moon because of the meeting she was currently ignoring. Well she'd be showing them a thing or two in a couple of hours because she had already made arrangements for the twins to spend the night with a couple of their nannies and she planned to make an appearance in the forest come hell or spell.

Made in the USA
Columbia, SC
03 July 2017